Also by J. Monique Gambles

Saturday's Epiphany: Reflections

When the Drama Has Ceased

Something About Ginger

Ballin' for Natalie

. . . Just a Season

J. Monique Gambles

Broken Ladder

For our community---

May we someday tear down stereotypes, embrace diversity and responsibly love one another and cherish the human condition.

Realizing that like any group or culture, behavior can either uplift or destroy.

Monique

TL,

Friendships should always matter.

Beautiful----

Either you know, or you don't. I know for a
fact, right now, and always, it would be you.

Lovely

Author's Note

This is a work of fiction. Any reference to actual events, real people, living or dead, or to real locales are intended only to give the novel a sense of reality and authenticity. Other names, character, places, and incidents are either the product of the author's imagination or are used fictitiously and their resemblance, if any, to real-life counterparts, is entirely coincidental.

Part I:

She walks in . . .

-One-

I lay there like a bawled up fist, the same fetal position for the last eight hours---lifeless, hopeless and broken beyond repair. Staring at the reflection of my self in the windowpane going over the lines again and again was how I was attempting to spend another Friday night.

But unlike all the rest of those Fridays I was going to fight that heaviness that held me captive and get up from that position. It was time to write again.

Two years had passed, and there were still no words--- no words dancing on my laptop screen or juggling in my head. Gone was the steadfast pecking of keys as I finished a novel or an impromptu poem. There was only one culprit for such a travesty: Something was wrong...something was broken.

Perhaps it was exhaustion from a meaningless job that zapped more energy than the impact of a nuclear missile hitting a stack of hay. Not to mention, spending countless hours with my therapist and psychiatrist, trying to find reasons as to why I had so suddenly lapsed into oblivion or what I hate to admit---depression.

I am Rebecca Claudette Moore: green-eyed, dreadlocked, slender, and a Jamaican Jewish girl who took her height from her mother, standing tall at 6" with all the right curves in all the right places. I lived quite simplistically. I was able to hold my own in my chosen profession, and at one time nothing seemed to bother me.

Up until this point, my life had been fairly good. I had written a couple novels that kept my bills paid, was physically fit, and wasn't involved with anyone. My job at the time as an editor for an offbeat, culturally diverse newspaper was perfect. In-between book signings and signing off on bylines and editorials, life just seemed to fall into place quite naturally.

I have a tough time figuring out just how and when things took such a drastic turn, causing me to loathe going into the office or doing anything that reminded me of work or the typical things people do at my age. I thought it was my chief editor, who worked my nerves with his haughty, pretentious, overbearing presence whenever he walked into a room.

Then again, it could have been the doorman, who seemed to grate my nerves like nails across a chalk board, acting as though we owed him something for opening the door each morning and evening - when I was more than certain that he was compensated quite well. Besides, my hands worked perfectly, even though they were having a tough time working on my laptop. His same tired uniform, stale breath, and uncombed hair - which was no doubt unwashed - drove me nuts!

And I dare not leave out the young, know-it-all recent graduates from SMU (some of my mother's former students), UT, and every other prestigious university of the fifty states who pissed me off with their simple stories and weird ideals. I took pleasure in shooting down their stories, which was probably my only solace. Their ass kissing made them think that that was all they needed to get ahead.

At the tender age of thirty-six - and not looking a day over twenty-four (even on a bad day) - I was hardly in the mood for their far-fetched stories and questionable research tactics, or better yet their character and absence of integrity.

My therapist seemed to think that I was too happy being single and that I needed to get laid; she was wrong. A lesbian no doubt but I was content on being single not happy. I was saving my money, making small investment deals, and writing until my heart was content – at least, until recently; besides I didn't need the emotional roller-coaster that seemed to accompany many of my previous relationships. As a matter of fact, it had been seven years since I'd sent my last partner on her way with tuition and her new lover - who I was sure, was going to beat the hell out of her one-day.

It was the depression that crept up on me just like it did for my grandfather. It was hereditary. My family and I knew all to well the crippling effects of depression.

As an only child, I was a natural loner anyway no-step siblings, questionable kin, crazy relatives, or dysfunctional parents. There was just the history of depression on my mothers' side.

Both my parents however were stable, hardworking individuals who showed me the importance of stability and family harmony. My mother was Jewish, my father Jamaican.

My Jewish side and I were extremely close and took very seriously our heritage and roots, which traced all the way back to 18th century Jewry. Being from Poland our religion was Judaism that was our Polish heritage, which explains my green eyes.

As far as my folks still in Mandeville and other parishes in Jamaica, I can remember clearly the wild, fun-filled parties, with the natives bumping and grinding to smooth reggae and soca rhythms all through the night. Just thinking about Jamaica brings on a sense of inner peace and relaxation; the seemingly endless white sand beaches, the lush countryside bathed in sunlight, smiling folk peddling their wares by the roadside and saying "no problem, mon" - making you almost believe it was true.

And the food - what excellent cuisine! Escoveitched red snapper, festival, ackee and salt-fish, pineapples, juicy mangoes, and sweet sugar cane from which white rum is made were all a part of me that I cherished and held sacred.

I remember coming home my freshman year in college, wide-eyed and talking nonstop about some girl (Judith), with whom, at the time, I was sure I was only infatuated. They discussed my experience with me, told me to practice safe sex, and sent me back to college life. They had raised a lady - no matter whom I decided to sleep with - and I have honored all that they taught me ever since (except for a brief lapse in my choices, choosing low-rent, needy-with-bad-credit, unstable women). Seven years of being single was heaven sent.

I was about to turn thirty-seven, my sex life was nonexistent, and menopause was more than likely not too far away. And, in spite of what my therapist suggested, I felt no need for any wild one-night stands, one-sided relationships, or being the sole breadwinner of any union! I had to deal with my depression and somehow turn things around.

In the attempt to rid myself of being glued to both my therapist and psychiatrist's state of the art sofas, I was going to get myself out of my funky mood and take part of my therapists advice and go to the local bar - the one I call "Cheers For Women" - *Suez.* I decided against the private scene because it would do nothing for my mood to hang with a bunch of folk who probably had more issues than I did.

I dressed rather quickly so I wouldn't change my mind, and arrived rather quickly. The bar had changed quite a bit since I had last been there it was bigger and had different feel to it. I made my way to the back of the bar and took up watching a game of pool. A cute red head brought me a drink that was sent to me by one of the bartenders who knew what I liked. I shot her a wink and lifted my glass.

I sipped on the Patron and peach schnapps and I began to feel my buzz almost immediately. I thought about how good life truly was; I was a professional, a published writer with savings, easy on the eyes, and able to hold a decent conversation.

My words, though, got caught in my throat when

she walked in; her side profile and the long tresses down
her back even made me do a double take - I mean, really,
how is someone beautiful from the *side?*

Creamy, milky skin, with distinctive features,
penetrating eyes, and pointy, perfect, soft pink lips that
glazed slightly with a smile – it all set me afire. She was
captivating as she walked, with confidence and sex
appeal, her friends following along in tow (which one
was she giving *all of that* ass to?) Beyond a reasonable
doubt, I knew that someone that sexy just had to be
taken.

I got back to the pool shark, *Cozy*, who continued
giving an ass-whooping, then excused myself to the ladies
room. A mess of toilet tissue and an overflowing sink
were minor nuisances in light of the fact that the mystery
girl was standing in the mirror on the phone in a deep
conversation, running her hands through her hair. She
nodded as did I and hurried to get out of there.

It was at that moment that I began to dream,
dream like it was my last dream and hope, like I had
never hoped before. I hoped that I could change her mind
and make her mine. I imagined that she would initiate
our first kiss, grabbing and kissing me like I'd never been
kissed before. I'd touch her in ways that spoke a special

language, and, during our first kiss, my tongue would savor the taste of her breast. Time would get away from us, and the next time we met I'd touch her, allowing my fingers to explore, knowing that just that easy we could simply screw. Then, I'd stop and back away (I hate it when women give it up so easily - it just turns me off). This one, I wanted to wait for until we could have sex, then make love. I wanted to love her; I had to hope.

-TWO-

I left the bar, grabbed a cup of coffee (it was going to be a long night), and headed to my refuge in Waxahachie. The drive down I35 was peaceful; it was a scary peace that foretold something looming ahead, and, though it would be painful, I would make it through. I was in cruise control at the perfect speed, heading in the right direction. Whatever it was, I would face it head on.

When I arrived at my lake front property, the one my parents gave to me when they purchased a beach house in Jamaica, I disarmed the alarm and headed straight to my office. I then cleared all of the clutter from my desk, sat in front of my computer, and wrote while the sun came up, rain fell, and the night came again. When it was all said and done, I had one novel completed, several bylines and editorials done, and a poem for my mystery girl, entitled "A True Dream."

My "getaway" or "refuge" where I spent time to write was nothing special only that it was by a lake. It was modest. My parents thought it would be a great place for me to indulge in my craft. They were right. Sometimes I'd stay there for days or weeks. It was quite crowded with the dogs but we managed. They slept while I wrote I slept while the stood watch and barked at night creatures that roamed. We'd pop in a George Benson CD and just coast through the day.

At about ten that night, I showered and climbed onto my sofa, then slept well past noon, missing Sunday Worship with my heterosexual friends. Except for my poem, I forwarded all of my work to my home email address, dressed, and headed back to Cedar Hill. Minus the coffee, I was still in a utopian state of mind, driving in cruise control.

With my novel completed, I knew I now had to face my agent, who had been leaving me message after message, wondering if I had anything she could shop for publication. I retrieved my cell from the console and dialed her up, and I wasn't too surprised when I reached her voicemail.

"Cindy, how are you? This is Claude, and I have a piece for you to take a look at. Maybe we can meet today or sometime this week. I know it's been awhile, but trust - this one is worth the wait. Give me a call."

She probably wasn't feeling me, considering I had promised her that I could get out 1-2 novels a year (which I had done initially) but, like I said, the previous two years had been a blur. Had I not seen mystery girl, I was going to request a leave for the remaining four months of the year and force myself to write something. My contract with Cindy's firm would be up by then, and at least I would have something to submit so we could end on a good note. I wanted to make sure I had fulfilled my obligations, even if it meant writing everyday until the sun came up for those remaining months.

Just as I was going to put my phone back, it rang.

"Hello?"

"Ms. Moore, how are you?"

"I'm well, and you?"

"Yeah, umm…listen, we really need to sit down and talk."

"OK, that's fine. When's a good time?"

"Immediately."

"Immediately, huh?"

"Yes, and you probably want to come into the office, say around one or so?"

"OK, I will see you then."

"Ciao."

"Later."

That was easy. I hurried up my pace so I could get home, let the dogs out, eat a little something, and print my manuscript out for my meeting with Cindy. I wasn't too worried about it being an unedited version because, knowing Cindy she could talk a publisher into looking at it just on her name alone. In addition, the software I had on my computer was so high-tech that it caught most of the grammatical errors.

I let myself in, only to be greeted by my two silver ghosts - my Weimaraners, Max and Moira. I let them out and watched them frolic in the hot sun for a sec before I got back on task in order to get ready to meet Cindy.

After getting a quick bite to eat and changing clothes, I grabbed what I needed to meet her and headed to her office in the Knox and Henderson Area. Excitement almost got the best of me as I sped down I45, and I found myself exiting off Knox and Henderson in no time. I parked and made my way to the tall glass-mirrored building. Surprisingly, the door guy remembered me (or was he expecting me?). Either way, he let me in with no problems.

I thought back to my reading of **The Alchemist** and immediately felt that I was surrounded by good omens. After taking the elevator up to the 14th floor, I quickly found Cindy's Office, The Euphoria Agency, and let myself in. I hit the small bell at the receptionist's desk and waited for Cindy to come from the back. Within moments, she appeared.

"Claude Moore, glad you could come on such short notice. Come back here," she said.

I strolled, happily following her to her office, excited about the completion of my manuscript and our long overdue meeting.

"Have a seat," she said, and suddenly I felt the tide change and those good omens run out the door!

"OK, let's see, our contract ends in, what, four months, and the last two years you haven't submitted anything for publication - does that sound right?

"Yes, I'm afraid it does, but I have a completed manuscript with me today, and I can have two more before the year's up. Is that OK?"

"Actually, that won't be necessary. Claude, let me give it to you straight--you have only one option: buy us out or relinquish ties, and I can probably get you fixed up with another lower-end agency, but I can't waive any fees to handle this."

"And what would be the difference? Either way, seems as though I lose money."

"Now hold on, Claude, you've been MIA what did you expect us to do here? We had a contract that you failed to honor."

I couldn't believe this. I felt like scratching Cindy's eyes out! I was being fired! I had a good mind to slam every door in sight and not comment on my "option". I was obviously perturbed by the sudden change in my fortune.

"Claude, to be honest, my associates wanted to sever our ties with you long before this meeting. We haven't heard from you in the last two years. They wanted to sue for breach of contract."

"And I would have counter-sued! I've been under a doctor's care."

"But," she interjected, "I convinced them that we have made a substantial amount from your books and that this was so unlike you."

"Yes, you have. PLENTY! I don't understand your position, you guys work with writers all the time; I'm sure you've had this happen before."

"Well, speaking for myself as a writer, I do understand, Claude. And, like I said, this was so unlike you. That's why I am willing to recommend you to another agency with very high accolades. But, it is your call."

The only "call" I wanted at this point was to call this broad all types of incompetent, half brained nitwits!

"What's the name of the agency, and do they market or sell what I write about?" I asked as my blood boiled. I swear if she didn't take her hoity-toity, all a sudden, lapse of a memory ass somewhere quick, I was going to scream.

"It's a new agency that is open to *your* type of literature, if that's what you're asking."

"Cindy, cut the bull crap! I'm not a closeted writer. My stories deal with lesbians – PERIOD, end of story."

"I'll tell you what, why don't you meet her? Her name is Angela Murphy of the Murphy & Taylor Agency. She's from Atlanta and has been in Dallas for a year or two, trying to build up her clientele. She's pretty good, from what I hear."

"This does not sound good, Cindy, and I must admit, I thought you and I were better than this."

"Claude, this is business. The *fling* you are referring too that occurred almost ten years ago has nothing to do with this."

She had conveniently forgotten the steamy nights we shared in between break-ups with our respective others. She had forgotten about the wild sex and the orgasms that had us both climbing the walls. Hell she had forgotten about the friendship that had developed as well.

"I'm a published author with more than five books in publication and let me repeat, they bring in a great deal of money to your company - why are you willing to push me over to a new agency that I know nothing about? This is crazy."

"You don't have to deal with this agency; it's just one that I think will suit you well. I would not steer you wrong. Besides, my agency is currently accepting only nonfiction and sci-fi stuff these days. Unless you want to write a steamy book about your many escapades, *kissing and now telling*, Angela's agency would be best. Your penetrating fiction novels that leave many people questioning themselves isn't what we we're pushing anymore, so in a way this was inevitable. I am glad you called when you did and things didn't get ugly."

"You could have called me sooner. Hell you could have stopped by! It's not like you don't have the address."

"I'm not going to argue with you Claude. This is business. Here is Angela's information. Give her a call and see when she can take a look at your latest work." She went to her desk and sat down thumbing through her Rolodex. My blood was still boiling.

"I've got to call her? This is great. What's the number?" I pulled out my Palm and patiently took down her information as Cindy called out the information. I was beside myself with anger, and I left quickly in order to avoid giving Cindy a piece of my mind and ruining my chances of being picked up by another agency.

20

-Three-

By Monday, I was hitting the snooze button by five a.m. and it was probably a total of ten times before finally forcing myself out of bed. Max and Moira were waiting for me at the back door, and I was glad that they were and that I wasn't greeted by the smell of dog urine or the harsh smell of their poop. Stumbling to the door, I let them out and went to start a fresh pot of coffee.

I washed my hands, went to the restroom to relieve myself, and brush my teeth, forgetting that I would have to wait on my cup of coffee; after brushing, the taste would be awful. I couldn't even sit on the toilet good before Max and Moira were back, wanting to play.

Begrudgingly, I went into the back yard and tossed around their toys until giving into a swim while they played in their portable pool; it's amazing how dogs often take on the habits of their owners.

I let the early morning summer breeze revive me as thoughts of mystery girl filled my mind. I knew it would be a lost cause because someone that beautiful surely had to be taken. Unable to resist, I fantasized about the two of us being a power couple with all the bells and whistles, living on a ranch-style property with four dogs, a huge pool, and not too far from the lake. I thought long and hard about her and what I felt like when she walked in; there was something about her that moved me - and later scared me - because I didn't even know her name.

My thoughts were interrupted when I heard the phone ring. I had no intentions of answering it, but I knew it was time for me to get inside and get ready for work. Ignoring the chirp from my old school answering machine, I walked to the shower, my wet feet hitting the hardwood floor. I peeled off my fitted, boy-short pajamas - only to see her face and my version of her naked body in my mind. She was beautiful and perfect in so many ways

But I knew my mind was just playing tricks on me, although it seemed so real; it was like her body was talking to me. Stepping into the shower, I adjusted the temperature and ignored my thoughts, hurrying to finish and head to my job.

By the time I left my house, it was around 7:45, and the morning traffic hadn't piled up yet. I zipped my red Jeep Grand Cherokee down I35 and made it to work by 8:15.

Once there, I closed my office door behind me and attacked last week's work, then took care of what I could for the week. And, whether I wanted to admit it or not, I knew I was revived. By lunchtime, I had completed most of the week's work, so, remembering my conversation with Cindy, I decided to call Angela Murphy; I had so many stories and half-completed books, there was no sense in not publishing them.

I placed my office phone on speaker and searched my Palm for her information. Just before I was about to dial her number, the familiar, annoying buzzing sound echoed over my phone, and my secretary said, "There's an Angela Murphy on line one, an Angela Murphy on line one."

I frowned a bit, wondering how she knew how to find me, and why the urgency.

"This is Claudette Moore."

"Good afternoon, Ms. Moore," she said in a smooth professional voice.

"Good afternoon," I replied, trying to tone down my concern.

"Ms. Moore, this is Angela Murphy of the Murphy & Taylor Literary Agency, and I understand that you may be looking for a literary agent in the near future."

"I am," I responded somewhat coldly before I could catch myself. I thought her voice sounded familiar for some odd reason, but I couldn't place it. We talked briefly about where we could meet and agreed to have dinner that evening at the Cheesecake Factory by North Park Mall - which, by the way, was exactly where I did not need to go, considering I was holding my own in the weight department, being so deeply depressed. I felt those omens again and couldn't figure out if they were good or bad, unsure as to whether or not my future agent would have my best interests at heart or be a bitch on wheels, in which case I would be doomed as a writer.

"How's seven-thirty sound?" she asked, snapping me from my crazy thoughts. I agreed.

Ending our conversation, I glanced up to see the "new girl" watching me intently. Rose, who was new to the paper, was from Idaho. We spoke in passing, but I hardly paid her any attention. As I read some of her articles, I gave her positive feedback and thought nothing of her until the moment when her bright eyes seemed to pierce through me like she knew something that I clearly did not.

"Can I assist you with something?" I asked as she pretended to look the other way.

"How are you?" she asked in that funny accent that I never could understand.

"Well, and you, Rose?"

"Just fine. Would you like some coffee?" she oddly asked.

"No, thank you."

"OK. Well, have a nice day."

"You, too."

Now, that was strange; most of the writers were so into themselves and their "gift" that they rarely spoke, not even at major functions. Of course, that could be attributed to the fact that I kept to myself, edited their stories, and kept the bull-crap to a complete minimum. I knew the game, and most uppity folk could not stand to see me as an author - let alone an editor - for this particular paper.

Well, enough about them. I had a very important meeting this evening, meaning I had to go home, pick up my manuscript, and swing back to the north side. I just hoped that I could leave the office by five and not have some last-minute bylines piling up with urgent deadlines.

I sifted through what I had and read as much as I could before taking a quick lunch and run at the YMCA; I knew I was going to need an extra burst of energy, not to mention mystery girl was on my mind heavy, and I had to avoid that forbidden place...it was too lonely, wishing for something I couldn't have. I almost sprinted my mile run, motivated by the notion that she was simply a tease and someone I would never see again.

I headed back to the office, arriving to find my pesky chief editor, Victor, on his way in with a wry look on his face; not what I needed right now, but I realized I had to entertain him.

"Claude," he said in his usually haughty tone.

"Sir? How can I help you?" I asked, very uninterested in his crap. I knew it had to be something serious since he came to my office instead of summoning me to his. I guess he realized that whenever he did that, I took my own sweet time.

"Were you able to get the bylines checked for Thursday's cut?"

Of course, that had slipped my mind, just like so many other things lately, and I found myself needing a good excuse as to why for the fourth time this year I would be late with our regular columnist and such.

"Yes, but it's Monday - don't you need them tomorrow by six?"

"Right. But Janie called and said you hadn't picked up her piece that you were to pick up Saturday."

"I'm on it. I'll have it done by tomorrow."

"Let me suggest something, Claude. Why don't you

let Rose help you so we can get this done?" Again, that haughty tone was ringing in my ear.

"Rose? Are you serious? Isn't she new?"

"She is, but she has some experience in editing, having worked at a local paper in Idaho."

"Right. Idaho - not L.A. or New York. I got this. You will have it by six tomorrow."

He sashayed out of my office, and I shut my door in complete panic. My memory was shot, which my therapist said was a sign of major depression. How I wished I could be on her couch right now or even under a table until everything blew over.

I had to devise a To-Do list. The first thing would be to reschedule my meeting, the second to swing by Janie's place and grab her work, and the third to stack up on coffee because it was going to be a long night.

My stomach suddenly felt like it was filled with bricks, and my office started to spin. I thought I was about to hit the floor when Rose walked in without knocking, asking if I was OK. I had to get it together quick.

"I'm fine," I replied. "Why do you ask?"
"Well, you seem a little pale, and you were holding your stomach when I walked by."

"I'm fine," I said, moving toward my office Plexiglas door, which damn Rose could obviously see through, hoping that she would take the hint.

"OK. Well, if you need some help, I can -"

"I will keep that in mind," I said before shutting my door.

I sat at my desk and proceeded to make all of the necessary calls, quietly praying for a miracle. Seeking strength in the hope I felt when my eyes gazed in my mind at the most beautiful woman I had ever seen. I let my thoughts of her transform me and transcend me to higher heights. And I knew at that moment that things were turning around and that there was still hope for me. For the first time this year, I would meet my deadline for our regular columnists - all seven of them.

I already had five completed, saving my most complicated and least interesting ones for last. One was geared toward gay teens (which I thought only addressed a small population of cross-dressers), and the other was advice on how to see the signs of a failed marriage. The latter, I felt had no place in our quirky offbeat paper.

It was Janie's piece, who I could have sworn I saw at a gay function, sipping on wine with some soft stud. Not to mention, her alluring eyes that seemed to want to ask me something whenever I picked up her articles. I called my secretary and told her to get Janie on the phone. Hesitantly, I picked up when I heard it buzz in.

"Hi, Janie. How are you?"

"Claude, how are you? I missed you this weekend. Everything OK?"

"Oh sure, just got a little caught up in something I was finishing up. I do apologize."

"Not a problem. I do understand. It's tough wearing two hats, you know?"

"Two hats?" I asked not realizing what she meant.

"Sure, you write and edit; that has to be a bit tough at times."

"It can be, but I usually keep the two separated. I just had an inspirational moment this weekend, and time got away from me. Can I pick it up this evening or do you want to email it to me?"

"Now, you know my superstitions and me. We can meet this evening. Tom is working late." Tom, her second husband, was my lawyer, whom I had hooked up with when I wrote my first novel.

"Right," I said, pushing an image of her and me from my mind. This whole business with Cindy and everything falling apart had me horny as hell for some strange reason.

Janie was a rare beauty, a Caucasian blonde with bright blue eyes classy, not sleazy. She was sophisticated and a true turn-on to anyone who saw her. Not to mention, she was quite wealthy and had her self together. I kind of felt like Tom married up; it seemed like he was some old country boy who came to the city to pursue his law dreams and landed perfectly with both the job and a rich wife who was probably ten years older than he was.

"I tell you what, let me swing by your place. I have to meet a friend in Cedar Hill at eight, so I'll see you say about 6:30?"

"OK. I should be home. I'll email my address. I guess you can MapQuest it?"

"Or I could use the navigation system in my new Benz that Tom surprised me with," she said with a chuckle.

"Why, of course; that, too. See you then," I replied and thought to myself, *don't you mean the one he bought for you with your money?*

"One down," I mumbled to myself and quickly looked at my Palm for Angela's number. I could only hope that she would understand that I would have to reschedule and that, if this were a reputable company, I wouldn't hurt my chances of being picked up in a major market. Right now, I was local, a Southern writer, and I wanted the big time from a bigger publishing house, like Doubleday, eventually turning one of my stories into a Lifetime movie.

"May I speak to Angela Murphy?" I politely asked, hoping not to sound unaffected by my decision to have to reschedule.

"This is Angela Murphy."

"Ms. Murphy?"

"Please," she insisted, "call me Angela."

"This is Claude, Claudette Moore. We spoke earlier."

"Yes, what can I do for you?"

"Something has come up, and I have to reschedule. I apologize for any inconvenience."

"Not a problem, but I really would like to meet before the week's up; the New Year will be here before you know it. Maybe I can come out your way?"

"Well, I have a couple deadlines, and I have to meet a client at 6:30 - and I don't know how long that will take. Sorry."

"I'll tell you what, I have an appointment at 6ish,

and I can swing by Cheesecake and bring dinner out there. It will probably be around 8, and if you still aren't finished I'll look over some of your stuff while you wrap up. Sound like a plan?"

"Sure, if it's OK with you?"

"Not a problem. Word on the street," she said flirtatiously, "is that I need to see some of your stuff and get you signed before someone else snatches you up."

"Is that right? Well, I guess I will see you at 8 or so."

"OK. I'll call when I am at the Cheesecake Factory."

I managed to get in as much as I could at the office, leaving half of one assignment and Janie's piece. I left, rubbing my eyes as I passed the new overachiever, Rose, who nodded as I got onto the elevator. It was 6 o'clock exactly, and I knew traffic would be unkind. Part of me wanted to cancel everything and walk into the office the next day with my letter of resignation, but I held off and thought about mystery girl again until forty minutes had passed and I was pulling into my driveway and waving at Janie, who had obviously beat me there.

"Sorry so late; traffic, of course."

"Not a problem. How are you?

"Well. You ready to work?"

"I thought that was what they paid you for?"

"Well, you know what I mean. Come on - and excuse the mess; I left the dogs out, and I'm sure they have torn the house apart."

"No problem."

I let Janie in, and she got her stuff set up in my office while I changed into some lounge pants and a muscle tee and grabbed a cup of coffee; I was certain it was going to be a long night.

Back in my office, Janie and I proceeded to read her column. I reached for my glasses as Janie went to fix a cup of coffee and chat on her cell phone. As I continued to read, I was somewhat taken aback; usually, her articles were about basic married life, but this one was different. It was a piece about married women secretly dating their friends. I got so caught up in the story that I almost shut off my editor hat. I felt like I was reading one of my novels, and all of the comfort that comes with the lifestyle was staring back at me.

The typical story of girl leaving boy for girl was staring back at me. It was the truth about falling in love with a woman, or a best friend, or co-worker that had my jaw dropping as Janie so eloquently put her piece together as though she was speaking from experience. My horniness was suddenly in full swing now and I wanted so bad to throw the things from my desk and passionately devour Janie. But I had better resist---- she was happily married.

I made changes to what I could when I could, but her piece was captivating, and I felt myself not wanting it to end. Was it true that Janie was, in fact, a closeted lesbian trapped in a loveless marriage? How did I miss this - if it really were true? My mind went on autopilot as I searched for other clues about Janie's possible hidden life, and how all of a sudden she was not only a character in my book - she was the leading lady. I could not resist.

"How's it coming?" she asked suggestively, standing in front of my computer, catching me completely off guard.

"Actually, this is really good, Janie; I didn't know you had it in you."

She smiled, "Yeah, well, there's a lot people don't know."
I looked up again, trying to read her, but I was clueless.

"Sooo, will you make the deadline?" she asked, coming over to my desk and sitting on the side of it with her thighs perfectly wrapped in slim-fitting jeans.

"I think I will. This was a lot easier than I thought."

"Yeah, it helps that it's familiar, huh?"

"Perhaps. So, what made you focus on a piece of this nature? Bored?"

"No. I'm not bored; interested, I guess."

"And Tom's take on this?"

"He thought it was rather interesting, too but what man doesn't?"

"Usually not the good ol' Southern Baptist, wouldn't you say?"

"Yeah, well, he knows who he is married to, and I'm a writer; there are some things that interest me outside of what is expected. I never hid that from him."

"I see." I said trying to erase the images of she and I intertwined like a pretzel on top of my desk.

"Who does your hair, Claude?" she asked, touching my locs and feeling them in her petite hands. It was like she wasn't afraid of them and that she could see they were a part of me, a walk and part of my heritage. My father and I both had them, and I remember when his dreadlocks became an issue at his work place and the lawsuit and settlement that followed. Yeah, our dreadlocks meant something to us.

"My stylist, Jackie." I sighed hoping that she couldn't read my thoughts

"Do you go once a week?"

"No, I go every two weeks. And, before you ask, they are a part of my heritage and me I am not Rastafarian.

Janie smiled as she touched the end of one of my locs. I couldn't fight it any more my insides were hot and I was moist. We looked deep into each other's eyes, and, before I could remove myself from the tense situation, we were all over each other. I savored the taste of her breast and lips and ran my hands through her straight blonde hair. For a woman well into her forties - or possibly fifties - her body was perky, and she was sensuous as she kissed me and explored my body in the center of my office floor. We didn't make it to the desk but our bodies gyrating against the carpet was sexy, sensuous and unforgettable.

It was the kind of sex that was rushed, not because we were hiding but because we both needed it. We tasted each other and were both so overtaken that we couldn't help having our bodies melt into each other before exploding in moans of pure sexual satisfaction.

Strangely without words, we dressed.

I then took one last look at her article and emailed it in to the news office. She left, after we shared a soft kiss, knowing that my agent would be calling any minute and that I had half of another article to digest before 6 the next day.

I moved to the next article with fervor, only to find it dull and boring and my mind drifting off to Janie and her sex. I started to call her back and forgo meeting Ms. Murphy when my cell phone rang. Angela was leaving the Cheesecake Factory and en route to my place. Not to mention, I had to remember that Janie was a married woman and completely not what I was usually into.

I showered quickly, put on my comfortable jeans and a modest button down, and put my locs up in a ponytail. After throwing on some flip-flops and splashing on some Carol's Daughter signature almond butter body spray, I went to my office to clean up the mess that Janie and I had made. There's nothing like the taste of a clean woman; I know Tom knew how good he had it.

I guess I know why she wanted to work on that article. Considering how she held her own, I was certainly not her first - and probably not her last. I had to smile, feeling as though something had been lifted from me; now, perhaps I would no longer drag my ass into work, maybe my poetry would dance across the paper, and my novels would no longer be so painful to write. Hope was more than just a mere thought.

-Four-

Sitting at my desk, I waited for my new literary agent (or so I hoped), thinking that by this time next year I'd have a more lucrative deal from a top publisher. The sound of the doorbell ringing was, in my mind, confirmation of what was about to take place; this was going to be my big break. I hurried to open the door, only to be taken completely by surprise at who was at standing there; I thought I would faint.

She stood there, as mesmerizing as she was when I first saw her. She was stunning, her tresses falling perfectly alongside her face. She greeted me with a smile that warmed my insides. It was her, mystery girl, *aka* Angela Murphy of the Murphy & Taylor Literary Agency.

"Well, aren't you going to let me in?" she said in a tone so familiar that I almost stuttered as I responded.

"Come on in, Ms. Murphy."

"Please, call me Angela."

I opened the door wider and held it as she walked in. With a soft white sundress with a low V-neck that showed the shape of her breast she was breathtaking. It tied around her neck in a small knot that seemed to compliment her small hands, ankles, and everything else about her. Even the sandals that showed her perfect toes, colored in a soft, dreamy peach, caught my attention.

"Let me help with that." I grabbed the large bag from the Cheesecake Factory so that she could adjust her briefcase across her shoulders, along with her small Louis Vuitton clutch.

"Thank you; I hope it isn't cold."

"Oh, I'm sure it will be OK. Follow me."

She followed behind me, I felt her eyes checking me out and all I could think was, *Damn! Why didn't I throw on something more professional, like some linen?* Instead, I was sashaying around in jeans and a button down.

"You look comfortable."

"Thank you. I just jumped out of the shower. I had to rejuvenate myself; just finished doing some work."

"Did you get it finished?"

"Most of it. I have probably one total left."

"Due tomorrow, huh?"

"How'd you know?"

"Our conversation earlier. I thought you were going to cancel."

"I started too."

"I know. Glad you didn't, though."

"Yeah, me, too," I said, remembering when I first saw her and where it was that I had seen her. I wondered if she remembered and if it meant that she was, in fact, *family*. The gay saying indicating that one was in the life of sleeping with the same sex.

"Your home is nice."

"Thank you. It isn't much, though; very modest."

"Is that what we are calling it these days?"

I had to smile, turning to look at her and seeing the smile on her face.

"Come on, let's eat before it gets too late. And, don't forget I have one more article to tackle, and I have to work out before I rest my head."

"Oh, so I guess I'm on a time table, huh?"

"No, you can stay as long as you like and take a look at anything you need to see."

"Well, thanks. I appreciate the invitation. I am very serious about acquiring you as a new artist." She winked at me as we sat and began to fix our plates to eat.

"I like the sound of that. I take it you brought a contract for me to take a look at?"

"One for you, and one for your attorney." A flirtatious smiled caused her lips to curve, and I knew the familiarity meant only one thing - maybe two: I wasn't going to get any sleep tonight, and this woman was going to change my life.

I could only imagine how she would. I poured some wine, and we sipped and ate our dinner over small talk, politics, and the future of our nation. The Iraq War, our sorry President who was on his way out, and the fact that being bi-racial offered not even an ounce of security.

She was mulatto, too, which actually shocked me because I was thinking more on the lines of Spanish and Black. Her thoughts were the same until she heard my accent, which rears its head every now and then. We talked about travel, dream vacations, and our family, and time quickly got away from us; before we knew it, it was well past midnight.

"Well, I guess I'd better take a look at your work. It is getting rather late."

"Yes, it is. Look at you already taking up all of my time - you gon' mess around and get me fired."

"And then you could work for me, full time."

"I see you already have this figured out."

"Oh, yes. I am hard at work over here."

"I guess we'll see."

"Yes, ma'am."

"Come, my office is on the other side."

"The other side? Is that your secret location or hideaway?"

"No, that would be the pool and Jacuzzi area, where I go to unwind."

"That sounds nice."

"It is. You'll have to come hang with me one weekend. Work permitting, that is."

"And I'll have to take you up on that - work permitting," she said with a wink.

"OK. What would you like to see first?" I asked as she sat on my couch and curled her legs up like she was ready for a nap. Her skin still glowed, and her smile still warmed my insides. I could get used to having her around. And, even if she were a terrible agent, I'd want her company, her friendship, and her companionship.

"Hmmm...let's see. I've read most of your published stuff, and that was pretty impressive. How about you jot down for me an outline of a book you'd like to publish in the future?"

I had to raise my eyebrows at her request. "You want me to do what?" I asked.

"Come up with a quick outline of an idea you have."

"I'll tell you what, why don't I write you a poem

and show you the outline that I was going to turn in to my last agent?"

"You sure? I mean, this could make or break this meeting."

"Listen to you. I'm sure. Take a look."

I handed her the poem that I had penciled in over the weekend after meeting her. I had to step out on faith, on hope, and on anything that I could find because she had awakened a sleeping giant. Only four or so hours ago, I was experiencing sex at a high altitude, and the conversation with her made me feel like pouring my Prozac down the drain and telling both my therapist and psychiatrist to kiss my ass - because I was back!

I watched her read the poem, showing no expression. I didn't know if it flowed or not. Her eyes seemed to run across each line. Yet, I still had to hope.

"This is rather interesting, and the motivation for this was...?" she asked with a smile.

"Can I plead the Fifth?"

"No." She said with a chuckle. "Wouldn't you want to impress your soon-to-be agent?"

"And who is checking out whom? I thought I was trying to see if I wanted you?"

"Really? So - *do you want me or not?*"

"Are you flirting with me, Ms. Murphy?" I asked, staring deep into her penetrating eyes.

"No, ma'am, and trust me - you will know when I'm flirting with you. I am merely asking if you'd like me to represent you or not?"

"Is this how you treat all of your potential clients?"

"Not all of them," she said with her trademark sexy wink.

"How about I take a look at the contract and have my lawyers take a look at it, and then we can go from there?"

"That sounds like a good idea, and besides, it's getting late. I know you still have some work to do."

"Yes, I do - and I don't have much time to get it done either," I said, pushing the vision of Victor The Horrible from my mind.

"You will. Do you mind if I take an outline of something with me and read it?"

"Not at all. I guess I will give you a call by Thursday?"

"Sure. That would be great."

"OK. Well, I guess I will talk to you then."

"Yes. Now, do you need any help getting your office and such straightened up before I leave?"

"Thanks for the offer, but I can manage."

"You sure?"

"I'm sure. Are you going to be okay getting home? It's after two. I have a spare room, you know. You can have it for the night. Or my room - it's going to be an all nighter for me."

"You know, come to think of it...do you mind if I use the phone first before I answer that?"

"No problem. Phone's over there, and I'll step out and give you some privacy."

"Thanks."

I slipped out of my office and started a pot of coffee. I knew time was getting away from me, and, no matter what, I had to come to work with everything done way before my deadline. I had to throw out the idea of wild couple hours with Angela, and that was probably harder to do than I would care to admit.

Her silky skin was dreamy and no doubt soft, as cotton candy that I knew would melt in my mouth. I had to wait, though; my job, which I loathed, was on the line, and the likes of Rose and my damn chief editor were probably taking bets that I wouldn't come through. I had to prove them wrong...I would prove them wrong.

"Everything OK?" I asked as Angela appeared in

the kitchen, obviously deep in thought.

"Yeah, just thinking about something."

I shook my head.

"Can I ask you something?" she said, leaning up against the counter.

"Sure."

"Did we meet before?"

"No."

"Are you sure?"

"Well...actually, I saw you this past Friday."

"You did? Your dreads are so much longer now from your other books. And were they up on Friday?"

"It's been awhile since I put something out; they grew, I guess. Friday was a tough day. I don't recall if they were up or not."

"Did you say something to me when you saw me last Friday?"

"No. I saw you when you walked in, and then again in the bathroom. That was it."

"Yeah, my business partner said you were there. I had no idea."

"It was me. I usually don't get out. First time I was out in about two and a half years."

"Why? If you don't mind me asking?"

"Just out of it, I guess. No real reason," I lied.

"How do the patrons treat you, considering you are somewhat of a celebrity?"

"Not a celebrity there. I've been going there for like fifteen years. I just blend in. That is, of course, when I do go."

"Do you really believe that?"

"Sure. Suez is like a *Cheers* for lesbians, *a place where everyone knows your name,*" I said, singing the familiar tune.

"Now, that's interesting."

"That's all it is to me."

"So, why didn't you speak last Friday? My partner says you noticed me."

"I noticed you? How so? I just saw you walk in."

"Let's see, her exact words were, '*She watched you all night.*'"

"Is that right? I don't recall. I left around 12 or so."

"Well, I guess the answer to your question would be 'Yes.'"

"I beg your pardon?" I asked.

"I would greatly appreciate staying in your spare room. I'm housed way on the north side. I wouldn't make it past downtown right now."

"Of course. Let me get you set up. Would you like some tea or anything before you retire?"

"No, just something to sleep in and a towel. That's all."

"That can be arranged. Not a problem. Anything else?"

"I'll try to look over your outline until I fall asleep."

I raised my brow, "And what makes you think you'll fall asleep reading it?"

Angela had to laugh, "You know what I mean."

"I know; just kidding. Come, follow me." I led her upstairs to my spare room and set out something for her to sleep in. I then set out toiletries in the bathroom and left her to get some work done.

I grabbed my cup of coffee and jumped back into my work. I gave it my all and finished at about 5 in the morning. I forwarded it to my work email address and saved backups on my travel disks.

I undressed, hurrying to take a quick shower so I could get at least thirty minutes' sleep. I put the shower on extra hot and washed as quickly and vigorously as I could. I closed my eyes and let some water trickle through my locs. Suddenly, a cool breeze opened my eyes.

"May I join you?" her soft voice said.

And, without saying a word, I moved to the side as she came inside, dropping the long nightshirt I had given her only hours before. Her body was everything I had imagined; her breasts were perfect with slightly dark nipples that overlooked a perfect stomach. I looked at her from head to toe and smiled.

"Does that mean you approve?" she asked as though she were reading my thoughts. This was absolutely the happiest day of my life! First I had Janie, now it was Mystery Girl.

"I do," I said as I pulled her close, her lips grazing mine and we looked into one another's eyes, then kissed. Her lips were soft, and she tasted like a mixture of vanilla and strawberries as our tongues wrestled with one another, consumed by incredible passion. We explored our breasts and took turns tasting each other. I allowed my fingers to play the piano inside her deeply, making music. Each stroke was extraordinary, touching the depth of ones soul. It was like going to church for the first time in years and the sounds of our music just seemed to quiet my soul. She climaxed in perfect tune almost holding a perfect note.

We slipped out of the shower, only to get intertwined on the sink, now sexing like it was the last bit of loving we would ever have. She moved into me with so much passion that we came instantly, then she allowed her tongue to explore me from front to back over and over again as we took turns tasting, sexing, licking, and sucking until we both exploded for a third time with so much intensity that it knocked us out and we lied there comatose on the bathroom floor until something jilted me from my slumber. Work.

I stroked the side of her beautiful face until she awoke with a smile.

"Hey, you."

"Hey."

"Everything OK?"

"Yes, ma'am," she said in her smooth tone.

"So much for getting to work on time, huh?"

"Oh, my gosh, that's right! You're late, aren't you?"

"Not too much; it's eight, eight-sixteen," I said, looking up at the clock. "I have to be there by nine at the latest."

"What about your deadlines? Did you get them finished?"

"I did. I had just finished before I stepped in the shower."

"Right. I did attack you, huh?"

"I wasn't completely innocent in allowing that."

"That's right. You could have said 'No.'"

"Never that. That would be foolish."

"Oh, listen to you."

"Way too good to have passed it up."

"Is that what you tell all the girls?"

"Don't deal with girls, and, no, that isn't what I tell all the women."

"So, there's a lot huh?"

"No, not at all. I'm actually single."

"Doesn't mean you don't have women."

"It does for me."

"So, why now? Why me?"

"You have to ask?"

"Yeah," she said, sitting up and looking into my eyes.

I didn't want to sound cheesy but I couldn't help it. This woman had me wide open. "I wanted you the moment I saw you. What about you?"

"I couldn't put your outline down. I was so wet after the first few chapter topics. My imagination went wild; I couldn't resist. Not to mention, you're kinda cute."

"Just kind of?"

"Yeah, just kind of. I like the locs, and your body is slammin'."

"'Slammin'? I haven't heard that term in a long time."

We both laughed. "Come on, you can't be late, and my partner is probably having a fit since I'm not home yet."

"Business partner?" I asked, trying not to appear jealous.

"Yeah, something like that."

"Hang on a second," I said, pulling her to straddle me, not allowing her to leave.

"You're going to be late," she whispered as I caressed her.

"I'm already late," I said as I began to kiss her. "I should have had you the first night I saw you."

"Better late than never," she said, kissing me back.

I pulled her close into me, kissing her and then her breast as she bit down on her perfect lips. She gyrated into me, and we became one motion until our juices spilled over, ecstasy filling the air. I wanted her in my world; I had a sexual connection with her that far surpassed any woman I had ever had.

I carried her to my bedroom and laid her down. I wanted to make love to her in my world. I forgot about work, deadlines, and anything that would cause me to stop. I let my locs fall to my face and pulled her half-wet hair down, too, running my fingers through it, then pulling it as I let my tongue explore her. Her moans were music to my dull world. She pulled my hair, too, allowing me to sex her with no rules, and for the next hour and a half we pulled hair and sheets, climaxed, and never spoke, instead letting our sex do all the talking in so many ways.

"Can I see you tonight?" I asked when we both finally had enough.

"Maybe," she said, teasing me.

"Are you sure just 'maybe'?" I said playfully.

"Business meetings that will probably run late. But, I'll call you this evening and let you know for sure."

"You promise?" I had to ask. There were so many things I wanted to do to her, let alone just be in her presence.

"I promise. You are definitely a keeper."

"I will be your lifetime." We were flirting, playing

with fire and getting caught up to quick--- A sure way to end any lesbian relationship. Moving too fast.

"You promise?"

"For sure."

"Sure you won't break my heart?"

"I wouldn't even know how."

"I'm going to hold you to that."

"By all means, please do."

"We better get moving, huh? I have to get home and set up for a couple meetings today. I'll continue looking at the outline and have Gillian, our editor, give you a call. You two can see when you can meet up."

"OK. And I'll have my consultants and lawyers take a look at the contract, and, if nothing else comes up, we'll discuss business by Thursday?"

"Right. Now let me wash up and get out of here."

"OK. You can use this bathroom, and I'll shower downstairs. I have to let the dogs out anyway."
We did the necessary and left out together with a soft kiss on the lips. I plugged in my cell phone and noticed a call coming in from the job.

"Hello?"

"Good morning, Claude."

"Morning. Who's calling?" I asked, knowing I was in trouble.

"Ah, we were expecting you over an hour ago. Everything OK?"

As much as I hated to lie, I did. "Oh, just running a little late, but I should be there in about fifteen minutes; had a minor emergency this morning."

"And you couldn't call, Claude?"

"Listen, I have my assignments. I overslept from my medication, that's all. I apologize. I'm coming off of 75 North right now," I lied again; I was really about fifteen to twenty minutes away.

"Come straight to my office."

"What about the meeting with Jenna and Sebastian?"

"Postponed until later. I'll see you in a sec."

"Bye."

Damn! He was working my nerves all ready today. Shit, I had just had the best sex known to mankind, and now I had to deal with his crap.

I exited the freeway, then parked and strolled briskly to our building. What could be so pressing today? I still had a couple hours before my assignments were due, not to mention that, even when they were late, my assignments were always perfect.

But, I guess none of that mattered.

The atmosphere in the office was chilled; more like a blanket of ice had made itself home to our once cozy work space, and I knew it because for once all of my crap was being thrown back at me. My office felt like it was no longer mine, and after seven years it was tired of me; I had overstayed my welcome. I could barely sit down before my secretary was sequestering me in the conference room.

I sat down my briefcase, turned on my computer, and pulled up the necessary files. I then printed them and headed to my doomed fate.

"Good morning," I said, walking into the conference room, which was filled with the top execs of the paper, my chief editor, and Rose – that, I couldn't understand, but I wasn't one to jump to any conclusions. I was here for the party, even if I were the one being roasted.

"Good morning," they all said in unison, and I had to hold back my smirk. I had never been let go off a job before, but I knew what this meant. I had had a tough two years, and while some will look at what you contribute and work with you, others are waiting for the perfect opportunity to send you packing; I guess it was my time to pack.

"Ms. Moore," my chief editor said in his same ol' nerve-wracking voice, "we have come across some information that does not sit well with our newspaper."

"I'm sorry," I said. I couldn't believe what I was hearing - and, more importantly, if that were the case, what the hell was Rose doing in this meeting?

"There have been several complaints from the workers here that you have been manipulative, a bully, and not a team player."

"Sir, with all due respect, I'm a senior editor here. I give each employee here undivided attention and take very seriously their contributions to this paper so these 'allegations' are absurd." I said motioning to what I liked to call a senseless nitwit with the emotional intelligence the size of a gnat!

"We are prepared to offer you a nice package in severance -"

"Wait a minute - I'm being terminated? On what grounds?"

"I believe I've just stated them," he said, annoying the hell out of me. I wanted *to choose* to allow 18 months of therapy to go out the window and kick his throat in and watch him choke on his own blood. It was obvious that he didn't give a damn about my contributions to this paper.

"Rose will be taking over your assignments, so I need you to make sure she gets the deadline work for today, and send to her the other stories. You do have the material for today's deadline?" He had to be kidding me. This was always the plan. I didn't even see it coming but who does.

"Yes, sir, I do. And, if that's all, I can get that for you right now." I proceeded to excuse myself as angered seeped through my skin. I wanted to slam doors and tell them all to go to hell; instead, I opted for the high road, cleaning out my desk and office behind closed doors. I forwarded everything I had to Rose.

I wouldn't allow them to get the best of me, and, more importantly, my folks had raised a lady; no matter how difficult this was, I had to hold my head high and accept responsibility for what I had failed to do, as well as the reasons why things had happened the way that they did.

I remember when my pops was laid off from the university as a janitor and my mother had to run the house. It ate him up because he was a man, a provider, but he was hurt, and there was nothing that he could do to save his job. He had to stay home and heal. The full Jamaican blood that ran through his veins wouldn't let him quit, though; he healed and decided to work for himself, cleaning as many buildings as he could until he could hire a crew.

He never quit, no matter what went down. My father was my role model. I knew I had to use this situation as a source of strength. I had saved up plenty of money, had a novel ready for publication, and hopefully a new agency that would put me on the map.

More importantly, I had Angela, and the quest to make her mine was more than enough motivation not to give up, throw in the towel, and quit on anything now.

I also made a mental note to contact Tom and ask him to look into my contract with the newspaper and double check anything that raised a red flag. I knew all too well the ways in which people discriminate, the dirty office tricks, the politics, and all the other bull-crap.

Part II

. . . I see her . . .

62

-Five-

Tuesday and Wednesday came and went, and there was no word from Angela; just the typical meetings with my former bosses and ironing out my severance package, which was quite lucrative. I also had meetings with both my psychiatrist and therapist about reducing my medication and eventually discontinuing my need to lean on either of them. I had even thought about booking a much-needed vacation to spend some time with my folks in Jamaica.

I sat in my living room, contemplating all of these things, when my phone rang.

"Hello?"

"Hi, sweetheart," came my mother's warm voice.

"Hey, Mom, how's it going?"

"Well, dear, how have you been?

"Pretty good, considering."

"Hmmm...'considering,' you say?"

"Yeah, just a sudden career change, I guess."

"Oh, you are finally going to write full time? Good for you. I told you you could do it."

"Well, it hasn't been set in stone yet, but more than likely that's the plan."

"And you should. Your father and I both think that you are more than capable, Claude. What's holding you back?"

"Steady income, for one."

"Oh, come on. Claude, you are such the cheapskate and penny pincher. You have a substantial savings, I'm sure."

"Yeah, Mom, but those things don't last forever. And, unless I'm some big time writer like Stephen King, I can't just NOT work."

"And what have we told you about comparing yourself to others? You have to live out your dreams and have some faith."

"I know. How's Dad?"

"He's well; going to the Islands on Friday to see your Uncle Peter. You know he's really sick; maybe you can go with him."

"Can't."

"Why not? It's not like you're working."

"Huh?" I responded, turning to look at the phone with my mouth slightly opened. She cleared her voice, trying to find a better response.

"Claude, you forget: although I'm not a writer, I have very close ties to the literary circle. When were you going to tell us?

"It just happened. I was going to call."

"When?"

"Mother, it isn't that serious."

"Claude, this is so unlike you; we used to talk about everything. This is major, and you don't call either of us?"

"You're right, and I apologize. It's been real hectic."

"Apparently, so listen, why don't you and I meet in a few hours at the school? Grab a bite to eat? Your Dad is working late."

"Sure, why not...not like I have anything else to do."

"And quit beating yourself up. What's done is done. You'd think your therapist would tell you that."

"Mom, enough already. Am I coming to your office at the school, or do you want to meet somewhere?" I was beating myself up because she was right. I let having sex with Angela get in the way of a deadline I had to meet. Not to mention I crossed the line sleeping with Janie, Toms wife.

"Let's say we grab some Mexican at the Margarita Ranch?"

"OK, I'll see you in a few. I'll call when I'm in the area."

"OK, sweetheart. I love you."

"I love you, too, Mom."

My mother always knew; it was like she had someone watching my every move. I mean, nothing went by her. You'd think she was some little old woman who sat around and listened to all the juicy gossip, but she wasn't. She was fifty-nine, vibrant, and extremely intelligent, and she knew things because she paid attention and could warm up to just about anyone.

I always thought it was so funny how she and my father hooked up. A Jewish woman from Brooklyn, New York, who was raised by her father, Samuel Ysorel, after her mother's untimely death, she began dating my father her last year of undergrad at NYU. He was a young, handsome Jamaican ten years her senior and was working as a janitor at the school. She spent countless hours at the library, and the two of them would talk during his break about their cultures and life in general. He'd talk about his folks back home in Mandeville and his father's objections over his coming to the U.S. and dropping out of college, and she'd talk about her issues with being her father's only child, a daughter without the hope of carrying on his family name.

My father had seven sisters and five brothers, and she enjoyed listening to his stories about how they grew up in Jamaica---one in particular the sounds of rain falling on their tiny home with the zinc roof during hurricane season.

She'd talk about Samuel's strict hand and his push to make her successful and follow in his footsteps. Samuel never disapproved of their union, in fact, he welcomed my father almost immediately, and his side of the family welcomed my Dad in, too. They married after dating for three years, then my mother began the Ph.D. program so she could teach history alongside Grandpa Samuel. How they had enough time to have me is something I'll never understand, but I guess Grandpa Samuel and my mother taught during different hours, so I spent a lot of time with him while my parents worked late.

Grandpa Samuel would fix my hair in two fuzzy balls with a crooked part for school, play checkers with me and told me plenty of stories about his childhood, and Jewish holidays and their importance. I can also appreciate a decent bowl of Matzo ball soup thanks to him!

My parents have been together ever since. When Dad was laid off, Mom decided to take the job at SMU so we could start over. Grandpa Samuel gave his blessings, and when I was just a little over six we headed to Texas. With a little help from family, my father started his own business and never looked back. I always think of the *Claudine* soundtrack with Gladys Knight and the Pips singing "Happy Home" because we sure had one. But it was during those times that I knew Grandpa was sick. He retired early when his depression took complete control of his life and by the time I reached my teens, Grandpa Samuel stayed curled up in the fetal position one day too long and drifted off, dying alone in his apartment. Mom was beside herself with grief but managed to show a good face and handled all of the affairs with no problems.

I began to prepare to meet my mother when I remembered that she told me my favorite uncle, Peter, was sick. Uncle Peter was a retired cricket player who had gained national recognition; a handsome single man who took very seriously the prestige of being one of the best in his sport.

I had been so out of it, I had not kept in touch. It sure would be nice to take a trip to see Uncle Peter and my folks. I could use a nice walk on the beach and let the sand slip through my toes.

I might as well; it wasn't like I had to be at work the next day. I texted my father and told him I was booking a flight and would meet him there.

I wasn't taking anything but myself, my laptop, a good book, and, my favorite flip-flops. It was an absolute must for me to go to Jamaica with only those things. I'd pick up clothes there and just lounge around. It wasn't like I was looking to meet anyone anyway; it was all about being with my family and eating my favorite Jamaican dishes, dancing and talking at the local roadside pubs or clubs with my relatives, going to a party that one of the rich neighbors was throwing, or even doing a little spoken word at the poetry scene there - that was always the best; it had been probably three years since I had read some of my poems there.

Not to mention, I needed the break. I needed to allow the hot Jamaican sun to rejuvenate my mind, body, and soul. And, perhaps by the time I came home Angela would have something to tell me, and maybe by then she would be feigning for me like I was for her. Her scent still seemed to cover my entire body, and visions of her climaxing danced daily through my mind.

The sound of my cell phone interrupted my

thoughts.

"Hello?"

"How are you?" she asked softly.

"I'm fine, and you?"

"Busy. What are your plans for this evening?" She said with a hint of excitement.

"Having dinner with my Mom in a few hours; that's it."

"Can you meet me at *Tryst*?"

"*Tryst*? Never heard of it."

"It's off 45 and Lamar."

"OK. Is it near *Brooklyn's*?"

"I believe so." She said as she cleared her throat.

"You OK?"

She coughed some more like she was a heavy smoker and I waited patiently for her to gain her composure.

"Excuse me---I do apologize still battling a little cold. And yes, it's by *Brooklyn's.*

"OK---What time?"

"There's a function there between six and nine. I'd like you to meet a few people."

"I can get there around seven. How's that?"

"That would be great. And have you looked at the

contract?"

"I have, and I spoke with my lawyer. It's airtight, but I'm sure you knew that."

"Well, we aim to please."

"Do you?"

"You can't tell?"

I had to laugh at her flirtatious nature. Certainly, she didn't think our sex was any indication that we could do business. In my mind, the two had nothing to do with one another; hell, I was looking for a girlfriend.

"I guess," I said, attempting to set her straight. I couldn't dare let her think that she had me wrapped around her tiny pinky finger...it was time I played hard-to-get.

"If my plans change, I'll call you."

"You do that. Talk to you later."

"Bye."

"Bye."

I had to let out a deep exhale; I had been waiting to hear from her since she left the other morning, and my insides were throbbing just from hearing her voice. I zipped to my closet and picked out something soft and sexy. I had less than three hours before I was meeting my mother, and I needed to haggle an airline for a ticket to

Jamaica. I wound up paying five and change and had to stay sixteen days instead of ten; oh well, I could use the time to unwind and try to get off my medication.

I made it to Margarita Ranch in no time and joined my mother, who was already sitting inside. I flagged down the waiter and asked for a cup of Green Tea.

"Claude, you're not having a drink this evening?"

"Yeah, just trying to figure out what I should have."

"You usually have a shot of Patron - that change, too?"

"No, I was thinking more like a glass of wine."

"Who is she?" My mother asked sitting back firmly.

"Mom."

"What? Every time you feel this sudden need to change, you've met someone."

"Mom, I'm single and I just lost my job. I want some Green Tea to unwind."

"Yeah, and Prince really isn't 4-feet tall - God knows, he just looks that short."

"Mom, where do you get those weird sayings from? I just want some Green Tea. That's it; a nice cup of tea - even if it is late August."

"You're my daughter, sweetheart. I've raised you,

and I know when you've thought you've found that perfect woman."

"Mom, you're crazy. How does Dad deal with you?" I said with all smiles.

My mother laughed. We truly had a great relationship. She knew me better than I knew myself. If I only listened to her more, I'd probably be better off in the relationship arena; I was just too stubborn.

"So, who is she?"

"No one," I laughed and motioned for the waiter to come take our cocktail order.

"I'll have a shot of Patron and a glass of white wine."

"I'll have a regular Margarita on the rocks. Thank you."

The waiter excused himself, and we continued to talk.

"You aren't a very good liar either, Claude."

"Mother, let it go."

She looked at me and smiled. "You've gotten yourself into something you can't handle, haven't you?"

"No, but I slept with Tom's wife, if you must know - and I feel like crap. Satisfied?"

"Claude, that's disappointing. I know you know

better."

"I do, Mom. It just happened."

"Let me guess…"

"No, don't do that. It just happened, and her name is Angela."

"Whose name is Angela?"

"The '*perfect*' one for me."

"I see. And how does Janie fit into all of this?"

"She doesn't. I think she was just using me for an article she's covering."

"The one about women leaving their husbands for other women?"

"That would be the one."

"Gosh, Claude; that's crazy."

"Mom, 'Thou shall not judge.'"

"And 'Thou shall not covet.'"

"Well, I didn't want her, per se; it just happened. It was a long time since I had some."

"Claude, be careful. You know the saying, 'What goes around comes around.'"

"I know. It won't happen again."

"I hope not."

"It won't."

"Now, who's Angela?"

"Possibly my new agent."

"And you're seeing her?"

"No, we just hung out and talked business."

"And I take it that's not all you two did…Claude, this is so unlike you."

"No, it isn't, Mom; I've been a 'hoe for quite awhile now," I said, emphasizing the word 'hoe'

"What?" she said, wide-eyed and sitting upright like she was about to die of a heart attack.

"Just kidding. You're right, it isn't my character at all."

"So, what now?"

"Nothing. We're supposed to meet tonight at a function and discuss the contract."

"Has Tom seen it?"

"Of course."

"And what does he think?"

"He says it is airtight."

"That's not good."

"Depends. But, in this case it's good for all parties."

"OK. So why the long face?"

"I like her. What else is new?"

"Claude, don't do it. Business and pleasure never mix."

"I know, I know. We're just meeting for business."

"Claude."

"Mom, I'm going to Jamaica with Dad for the next couple weeks - how much trouble can I get into? By the time I come back, she'll be history in my thoughts."

"So, you are going?"

"Yeah. I gotta go check on my favorite uncle."

"Well, that should do you just fine."

"Are we eating, or just having chips and queso?"

"Well, I plan on eating."

"I'll just have some chips."

"Do you see this? Guilt has your stomach in knots right now."

"I don't feel guilty. I just want to see her."

"Oh, Claude. What am I going to do with you?"

"I know. I'm going on thirty-seven; you would think I would have a better handle on this stuff."

"Well, if you'd just listen to your mother, you might."

"Mom, you've only dated my father - what makes you so experienced in love?"

"You're kidding, right?"

"Well?"

"Well, what? Your father and I dated, but there

were others before him. I chose him out of a couple - one in particular, a Jewish settler, who's worth a couple million right now."

"Really? So you mean I could have had a white father?"

"No, your father is who makes you who you are. What I'm saying is that I could have had a whole other life. I chose the man who was best for me, and not what would have looked good to others."

"No one knows about Angela."

"Probably not, but I'm guessing you are choosing her because she looks the part."

"Not at all; we had a connection. It was rare."

"After the sex, or before?"

"The moment I saw her, I knew I wanted her."

"Be careful, sweetheart."

"I love you, Mom. You are always there for me, even at the age of thirty-six."

"Well, that's what mothers do. Now go, go be with Angela; you're not going to be much company today anyway."

"Are you sure?"

"Sweetie, go on. I'll be fine."

"OK, let me drink up. And tell Dad I'll call him

before he leaves in the morning."

"Will do. Kiss--- Kiss."

I reached over and kissed her warm olive skin. My mother was a rare gem; so wise and wholesome. There was nothing I couldn't talk to her about; she was my best friend. I finished my drink and excused myself, heading to Tryst to see what Angela had planned.

-Six-

The parking lot was packed. When I drove up and saw many of the female patrons hanging over the balcony outside, I imagined it was going to be eventful. I parked and walked to the club. My cream linen outfit and matching sandals seemed to glisten in the evening sun.

I spoke to the attendant at the door and followed behind a group of younger Caucasian women. I held back laughs as one of them proceeded to tell of a disastrous blind date and how she was at her wits end, about to go back to the "other side." "Seriously," she chimed, "what do I have to lose when so many women now are damn near cross-dressers? Ever since that damn *Shane* on the *L Word*, everyone wants to be some butch. I might as well date men!"

I guess she was somewhat correct. The new look was something to ponder. Everyone wanted to play the "stud" role, and it had nothing to do with anything except perception. I longed for the days when the women were so beautiful and your jaw would drop when you found out that they were, in fact, lesbians who wanted to look like and be with other women. Angela seemed to fit the bill of what I had so desired.

I carefully walked up the rickety stairs and decided to page her. By the time I reached the top of the staircase, it felt like I had reached the Promised Land. It was wall-to-wall with beautiful women of all shades. I saw white, brown, tall, short, professional, trendy, straightened hair, natural hair, locked hair, slender women, voluptuous women, butch women, and my jaw just dropped...well, not exactly.

I almost regretted paging Angela; I wanted to check out the scene, which obviously had been going on without me. I had to have another drink. I moved through the crowd, brushing against one beautiful woman after the next, keeping my composure and smiling when necessary until I reached the bar. There another dreadlocked sister, with bright beautiful doe eyes and smooth cocoa butter skin, greeted me.

"Hi, I'm Gillian. What can I get for you this evening?"

"How are you? I'll have a shot of Patron and a Martini, dry." I couldn't believe she said her name before taking my drink order.

"OK. Coming right up," she said in a sultry voice.

While she fixed my drink, I turned to surf the crowd to see if Angela was in its midst, and there she was, standing there with a sexy black dress on, holding a glass of wine, talking to a couple women. It was evident that she was working the crowd because everyone looked attentively in her direction. I smiled; her presence was powerful.

"Here you go," Gillian said, interrupting my thoughts.

"Thanks," I said, trying to get back to watching Angela. She was so smooth and sexy conversing with her entourage. I watched as I sipped my drink, thinking of her and the encounter we shared. My body simmered as I watched her attentively; it was my hope that I could whisk her away from here.

I sighed deeply and worked my way through the crowd of beautiful women. I figured Angela and I weren't going to spend "quality time" this evening, so I convinced myself that after my drink I would slip down the same rickety steps and head on home. I knew I had to pack and mentally prepare for the long plane ride to Jamaica.

The haze from the smoke-filled club pulled me into a trance while I searched the crowd for a restroom, and I finally found one beside the other end of the bar. Surprisingly, it was clean, and my first thought was to splash my face with cold water so I could wake up from

my damn fairytale of living happily ever after with
Angela, but instead I looked in the mirror and took in the
sadness that filled my face and the desperation that filled
my eyes.

I thought a few orgasms were enough to fix my
issues or cure me of the depression that had clouded my
life for the past couple years, not to mention the loss of
my job, career, and just about everything that made me
the writer that I thought I was destined to be. I was
thinking of throwing in the towel when the door opened,
and Angela, in all her beauty, stood beside me, grazing
me with her beautiful soft skin.

"Hey, you," she cooed in a sultry voice.

"Hey yourself, stranger," I said, attempting to hide
my green face, which I'm sure was again, evident.

"Now, is that any way to greet the woman that
holds your bright future in her hands?"

"What's up?" I said, turning to reach for a paper
towel. She stopped me, grabbed my hand, and held it at
her side. I turned to her, and she softly kissed my full
lips. I wanted to melt like butter in a scorching hot frying
pan right there on the bathroom floor.

"I miss you," she whispered, then kissed me again,
this time allowing her tongue to taste mine.

I pulled out all the stops and kissed her with all the passion I had in me. She grabbed my face, then we kissed some more until she pulled away, wiping her pouty bottom lip and looking at me, almost possessed - like she wanted to rip my clothes off right there in that vibrant, fluorescent bathroom.

"Let's get out of here?" I asked her with a look in my eyes that told her, *I would sex you right here if I could.*

"I can't; it isn't polite for the hostess to leave."

I sucked the bottom of my lip, more out of frustration than anything else. I wanted this girl; it was her, and that was it.

"I have to get going; early morning. What time does your event end?"

"A little after nine," she replied, looking at the dainty Movado that sparkled on her tiny wrist.

"Why don't you stop by when you're done?"

"I'll see what I can do."

"I see. Well, I leave in the morning around 5. My flight leaves at 7:30."

"Flight? Are you going on a vacation without me?"

"That depends. You can join me if you like."

"And where would WE be going?" she asked with a

sheepish grin.

"Home. I need to see some of my folks."

"Jamaica, huh?"

"Right."

"Well, I may have to join you," she said, reaching for my hand and twirling it in hers.

Our private meeting was interrupted when a group of *modelesque* young ladies came in, and, of course, Angela did the meet-and-greet thing. I quietly slipped out of the bathroom and her presence and made my way to the door.

-Seven-

I tossed and turned the entire night, wondering why my phone hadn't rung or why my doorbell didn't ring. My mind kept drifting back to our wistful meeting in the restroom. The taste of her soft lips and the way she touched me; it was so caring and warm. I finally gave up sleep at around midnight and decided to get up and work around the house, as well as get my dogs ready to drop off at my mother's. After packing their bags, I packed my things and prepared my home for my long departure.

I arrived at the airport with plenty of time to spare and went through the arduous task of going through check-in and receiving the "all clear" from the stout clerk. I found my way to my gate, then looked through the boarding area for my father, who had left in his own car with my mother. I thought for sure I would see them prior to getting through screening, but I hadn't. But knowing Mom, she did the typical kiss, kiss in the car and left immediately as my father made his way to the check-in area.

With little less than an hour before departure, I went into the empty newsstand and purchased the latest Essence, Ebony, (the magazines for women of color) and

Women's Fitness magazines. I glanced down at the variety of candies and turned away, trying to stick to my goal of cutting out candy, junk food, and sodas; my medicine seemed to require it. I handed the Middle Eastern cashier my twenty and watched her carefully so I could concentrate on my change and not the tempting Fifth Avenue candy bars that were teasing me.

As I grabbed my change and put it away, I reached for my phone and texted my mother, telling her I loved her and I would see her soon.

"Claude," my father called out to me as I walked out of the newsstand and fumbled with my phone.

"Hey, Pops."

"Av grab the New York Times, eh?"

"I did not. My apologies, Pops. Let's get one."

I adored my father. With his smooth cocoa skin and pearly white teeth, his features were strong and a true resemblance of his Jamaican heritage. His long dreadlocks, which looked Rastafarian, hung below his shoulders. He was a short man, yet built like a gazelle. He didn't have an ounce of fat on his body. We shared the same thick lips and rounded nose.

His story was amazing. His family in Jamaica was very poor by American standards. They were educated under the tough British standards and many of his sisters and brothers studied education, and went on to be teachers there in Jamaica. Some were in law enforcement and some farmers except Uncle Peter. Uncle Peter was special in every ones eyes. He was an international star in the sports world of cricket.

My father dropped out of teachers college against his father's wishes and applied for a visa to study in America. He was granted such but soon after he arrived dropped out of Queensboro College and married an American so he could stay. After two years they divorced and he began working at NYU as a janitor. He planned to apply but had to go back to Jamaica to visit my dying grandmother. He was the oldest son and considered a strong presence in his family. Next to Uncle Peter he was the one responsible for his family's success.

"Me get it for you. Me ere you out of work deeze days, eh?"

I smiled at his sarcasm. "Yeah, but I can mange to pay for a fifty-cent newspaper."

He smiled at me, and I went back into the store to get his paper. I grabbed two Fifth Avenues and rationalized that I was about to go on vacation - so I should be allowed to eat what I wanted. Besides, my aunts and uncles were going to feed me nonstop from the moment I got off the plane.

"One newspaper for the old man."

"Me no old. Gwan gal and git eh plane."

"Age before beauty, Pops. Lead the way."

"Gate seventeen. Eh, gal."

"Yeah, mon" I said in the traditional Jamaican accent. We walked to the gate, talking about the news, our President and the Iraq crisis, and the upcoming elections in Jamaica. Our conversation carried onto the plane. Clearly, our age differences were at odds. I thought the new party, JLP, should be a clear winner, while he thought the PNP was the better of the two because of their experience. He had good points, as did I, and we laughed as much as we could, poking fun at each other's party of choice.

There was so much that was to be done in Jamaica, but clearly the two parties were at odds over the future of such a beautiful country. My heritage was riding on this vote. The violence in Kingston was spilling over into our parish, Manchester, and many of the other parishes were taking the brunt of the drug traffic-kiting. The cops in Mo bay were having a time with the drug lords, shooting them down in their tracks. It seemed as though no one cared any longer, and the current administration was in denial of what had become of Jamaica.

Our family members still in Jamaica feel torn in a country they love so much and called home. Only a few have left to work in the states, one died from a car accident the week after arriving and my dad who was faring pretty well while the rest have stayed. My father goes back at least twice a year to tend to business and the land we still have in Mandeville. And, each time he returns home, there are more changes, more violence, and more sadness in his eyes.

I let him read his paper and turned my head against the window to get some sleep. The three-hour flight was getting away from me, and before I knew it we would be zipping through the airport to meet my cousin, Sean, who worked for Immigration, and my other cousin, Jonathan, who was a police officer, whisking us away into my father's car, which he kept there.

I awoke as the plane touched down. Stretching like I had just awakened from a five-year slumber, I gathered my belongings as soon as I could because the moment we made it through Customs as citizens, we would be off and running. As the plane stopped, all the passengers rose to their feet and scurried off with small bags in tow and warm smiles on their faces. As we walked through the long terminal, I gazed at the beautiful pictures of Jamaica's rich history and its folk singers while my father talked on his phone.

With no bags to pick up from the bag check area, we headed to Customs, where we were greeted by my cousin, who quickly gave us hugs, stamped our passports, and sent us out to the parking area with my father's keys. I dreaded the left-hand roadway but sucked up my complaining because, in a sense, I was at home. And, no matter how Americanized I was, there was something about Jamaica that brought out the best in me.

I remembered our trips both when I was growing up and well into my teens, when we would visit relatives throughout the parishes and eat island food, such as cooked ackee fresh from the tree, breadfruit, juicy mangos, and chocolate tea.

The beautiful sun and the smell of coal burning in the air was dreamy as we left the Montego Bay airport and drove through the streets to the back roads, which led to Uncle Peter's house in Spanish Town. His modest home on a hill seemed sullen and sad as we pulled up. I could remember when he would meet us at the front gate with smiles and warm hugs.

I felt sadness because I knew Uncle Peter was at death's door. We parked, and my father wrestled for the key and let us in.

"Hey, Uncle Peter."

"Im no ere; im en eh hospital. We gwaan see im later. Me gwan git papers en such."

"He's that sick? I thought he was homebound."

"Claude, me no said im ere en dah first place. Im en deh ospital. Yuh see im soon."

"Dad, I just asked a question; cool down."

"Es eh dumb question. Peter sick. Very sick, Claude."

"I know. That's why I came; I wanted to see him."

My father rolled his eyes up, and I had to wonder why he was in such a sour mood. Uncle Peter was his youngest brother, and since both my grandparents had died some time ago, my father handled a lot of the affairs in Jamaica. It only seemed fitting that he would be here for Peter, just like he was there when my Aunt Mary was sick.

Uncle Peter's house was stale, and his lavish furniture seemed dull without his presence. The huge cabinet that housed many of his medals, trophies, and recognitions seemed like a faded memory. I could only wonder why; Uncle Peter was a world-class cricket player, and there was no one here to greet us, prepare food, nothing. I had a notion that my father was hiding something, but given his sour mood - which wasn't typical - I went against asking him what was truly wrong.

We were in and out in no time, then my father locked the doors and gate, and we got back on the winding road that went towards our home in Manchester County.

"What about the hospital, Dad?"

"Me ah go tomorrow. Me gwan to Mandeville."

"Well, drop me off at Aunty Carol's. I'm not ready to go to Mandeville yet."

"We yah go, Claude?"

"To Aunt Carol's in St. Mary's."

"No, ah go dere Claude. Me ah go to Manchester."

"Dad, what's with the attitude? You have your agenda, and I have mine. Now, drop me off."

He did.

Those were the last words I said to my father that trip. He dropped me off at Aunt Carol's, waved, and drove off. I flopped down on Aunt Carol's sofa and fought back tears like a ten-year-old child. I had never seen my father act like that before, and it was terrifying.

"Yuh fader going tru something awful. He no wan urt yuh, Claude, wit Uncle Peter's misfortunes."

Not understanding a word she was saying, I excused myself and washed from the long flight, then sat under the huge mango tree in their yard and waited for some of my cousins to come through and take me out. Tonight - and for as long as I wanted while in Jamaica- I was going to partake of some of the best weed known to man. My father was acting like a madman, and I wasn't letting him and whatever he was dealing with bring me down any further.

By the eleventh day there, I was damn near Rastafarian, smoking weed, drinking Red Stripe, and eating red snapper, cod fish, salt fish, and anything Jamaica had to offer. I sat back allowing the sounds of some of the dub poets anger me and rile me up for a revolution. I was angry, angry with my father.

I let my sweaty body and funk along with my un-kept dreads symbolize my frustrations and anger. In an aberrant state I walked to and from the local patty shop, grabbing a patty in a heavily, grease soiled, paper bag and a red stripe and with a look of anger on my face that screamed REVOLUTION! I almost wanted to pump my fist but was worried that they would lock me up thinking I was the mad man!

When I decided to finally turn back on my phone, and I had almost sixteen text messages, a bunch of forwards, and well wishes, including one from Angela that simply stated, "Pick me up from Montego Bay Airport on the 4th. I'm stepping out on faith."

I stumbled from my room and asked Aunt Carol what was the date.

"September tird eh," she said

Shit, I had less than twenty-four hours to meet her, and I looked a pure mess. I called the beach house we had on the private beach in Ocho Rios and booked it for five days. I told the property manger to call me if my father decided to come down, giving her my cell phone number and a guarantee that I would pay for her assistance. She told me she would do so, but she was almost positive he had been there almost a week ago and had said nothing about coming back in the next five days. *Bastard.* Uncle Peter lie sick in some hospital, and his ass was vacationing at the beach house.

Aunt Carol kept saying that Uncle Peter was 'obeah' and uttering strange things, at times incoherent, so I knew visiting him wasn't going to happen. That 'obeah' nonsense was one thing I had no tolerance for. Aunt Carol told me to let him rest it off and wait for the doctors to give us the OK to see him.

Uncle Winston drove me to Montego Bay the next morning, and I rented a car (American made) and waited for Angela, who was arriving on the first flight, a little after eleven.

96

Part III:

97

. . . we fall in love. . .

-Eight-

We left Sanger International Airport and headed for Ocho Rios. My insides warmed up the moment she walked from the terminal in a white sundress and leather sandals. Pulling her carry-on, she smiled at me, and we embraced like two long lost friends.

"Good landing?"

"Superb. How are you?"

"Great. So glad you could join me, Ms. Murphy."

"Likewise," she said with a wink.

"This place is beautiful."

"It is. Wait until I take you in through the countryside and you can see all that Jamaica has to offer. It's somewhat peaceful, and there's a sense of serenity here. Amazing."

"Well, I look forward to my tour."

"Come, I want to show you Fern Gully, and then we will head to the beach. Did you bring your camera?"

She smiled innocently, "I forgot it."

"No worries, mon, meh give you an experience that you will never forget."

"Please, by all means do so. Urgently."

We both laughed at the connotative conversation

and held hands while I drove through the winding roads down to Fern Gully. Angela was mesmerized at the ferns and roots that seemed to reflect a Rastafarian heritage, as well as the coolness of the air and the burst of sunshine when we turned onto the main road.

"This is absolutely beautiful."

"We're going to go by Dunn's Falls after we settle in, then go by the pizza shop there in town."

"Pizza? In Jamaica?"

"Sure. The bread here is on a totally different level. You'll love it."

We pulled into the private villas that overlooked the beach. I checked in quickly, and we headed to our bungalow, which sat overlooking the beautiful white sand and ocean.

Our maid told us she was at our service and could cook any of the island dishes that we'd like. I told her perhaps tomorrow I'd bring in some ackee, breadfruit, and saltfish.

Ignoring the sea calling us, we dressed for the falls and made our way there. There were tons of tourists and people from every part of the world there. We paid the Jamaican price because I made sure I spoke in an accent, polishing up my patois for just such occasions had paid off.

It was six hundred feet of rocks and cool river water. We held hands with an Indian family and made our way to the top. We drank bottles of water, partook in authentic Red Stripe, then headed back to the car.

With pizza to go and two cases of Red Stripe, we went back to the villas, sat outside, and sipped before changing into our bathing suits. Like two sisters, we tanned for a moment, then went for a walk and reserved two jet skis. It was refreshing, feeling the salt-water splash onto my face. My heart raced as I went further and further, then turned and headed back to the shores.

"That was breathtaking. I can't remember it being so much fun."

"Yeah, it's pretty fun. Tomorrow, we'll go out on the boat for awhile."

"Sounds like a plan. I can't wait."

"Come, let us go inside and unwind," I said, sending her a wink.

She winked back, and we let our shoulders touch as we walked back to the beach house. We both had one thing in mind, and that was allowing our bodies to touch and melt into one another. I knew the maid would be gone and we could make love all over the beach house uninterrupted.

"You thinking what I'm thinking?" she said with a hint of sexiness that almost made me melt.

"Yeah, you ready for a nap?"

"Haha…not exactly - but you might be ready for one after I get finished with you." She said then winked.

I laughed. I wanted her so bad, I could taste it.

"Come on, you are walking too slow."

"Well, I'm enjoying the feel of the sand in-between my toes and the cool breeze."

We both laughed and made our way into the beach house.

"Can I sex you?" I asked, pulling her into me, letting my mouth melt into hers. It was suffocating and an utter pleasure to savor her lips and tongue, then her breast, removing her bikini top.

"Are you asking or telling me?" she said in-between kisses.

"I'm telling." I pulled off the rest of her bikini, tasting all of her as she moaned. I tickled her insides slowly, then faster as she gyrated to my rhythm, listening as she climaxed and trembled against me. I led her into the room, and we made love for hours until the sun peeked over our shoulders and we fell asleep tangled up in our sweat and juices. I wanted so much to watch her sleep and listen to her heart, hoping that it was beating for me. But, sleep hit me like a tidal wave, and I was fast asleep in no time. My dreams were of her.

I woke up to the vision and pleasure of Angela straddling me. Her breast were perfect and as bright as the morning sun. Gripping them, I moved into her, looking deep into her eyes as her long tresses hung alongside her face. Moving with assured intensity, we looked at each other, with me loving her loving this. I let my hands grasp her buttocks moving my fingers inside as she moved into me, and we sexed until she exploded first, arching her back and trembling.

Angela slid off me, then tasted me for hours; simultaneously, I came while moaning her name and telling her, "I love you."

Pulling her hair while she tasted me, I said again, "Did you hear me?"

She stopped and looked at me, softly stroking my clitoris.

"Can't you tell how much I love you?" she licked me and went deep inside, and I let go and let nature take control, having the best orgasm I had ever experienced. Trembling and taking a cool breath, I pulled her up to me, kissing her and playing in her long tresses.

"I need you."

"I need you, too."

I was on top of the world! I met her, got her, and was having the best sex of my life. As superficial as it all sounded, I was still on top of the world. It amazing that as humans we equate good sex with love. I was guilty of all of the above.

"So, what shall we get ourselves into today?" Angela said, moving her hair behind her back."

"Let's start by putting the 'DO NOT DISTURB' sign on the door."

"Are we going to be naughty all day?"

"Do you oppose?"

"Oh, of course not; I can do this forever."

"Forever, huh?"

"Yeah, you can be my forever."

"We should go down to Mexico next weekend and go Salsa dancing."

"Salsa, huh? That would be nice; we can do that. I can see us going to Mexico."

"OK. Mexico it is."

"Now come make love to me."

"I thought you would never ask." I pulled her close to me then whispered into her ear.

"You're so damn sexy.

"Sex me," she said softly as I kissed the small of her back and placed my toy inside her. I grabbed her hair as she moved with me and let my tongue play around her rotund buttocks. I was never into role-playing with any of my other exes. We had simple "missionary sex" if there is such a thing in the lesbian world. But Angela brought out the beast in me and tapped into my inhibitions. I wanted to explore everything with her ever since our first sexual encounter.

"You taste so good."

"You like it?" she purred softly and like cotton candy, she melted into my mouth.

She moaned, and I let my tongue make circles until she came. Hoisting myself into the contraption that slid up my legs and rested above my hips we explored the world of sex. We sexed from behind taking turns, and using condoms only when we switched who would wear. We laughed, giggled, purred and had the time of our lives in between hot, forceful kisses until we both climaxed. Collapsing, we cuddled and began to talk. It was time for the "talk" and time to make things official.

"I can love you for the rest of my life." She said tracing my lips and staring into my eyes ever so gently.

"You can?" I asked, playing with her hair.

"Yes. I've needed this security for so long. You are my lifetime."

"And you are mine.--- I don't want to leave this place."

"Me either." WE were making the same dumb promises that only lasted as long as the smell of sex stayed in the air.

"You're not going to wait and tell me you have some girlfriend back home are you?" I asked.

"My girl is right here with me." She said as she rested her head against my breast.

"You promise?"

"Yes. It's you and only you. My last girlfriend is long gone. What about you? Any secrets?"

"No. I was single until now. My last girlfriend is a memory I'd like to forget. I need this. I want this."

"And you shall have this."

"What about our business deal?"

"Shouldn't be a problem. We do business, and we have a relationship; I don't see that as a problem, do you?"

"No."

"Katrina will just have to adapt."

"Your business partner?"

"Yeah. The one and the same."

"Did you guys date before?"

"Something like that, but it was horrible. I probably had the worst years of my life with her."

"Really?"

"It was rather dramatic and chaotic and not something I want to relive."

"Is it difficult being business partners?"

"Not lately. She's finally got an understanding of us not being together anymore and me moving on."

"Good, because I want you all to myself." I said pulling her into me.

"And you shall have that."

"I love you."

"I love you more."

The rest of our vacation was spent making love, taking long walks on the beach (sans holding hands), and talking about our plans of being the premier power couple, as well as our future together. It was her; she was what I had been waiting on all my life.

"We have to come back here next year and celebrate

our one-year anniversary."

"OK. That can be done," I said as we packed our bags and headed back for the states.

-Nine-

My mom was at the gate when Angela and I walked out behind my father (my father, whom I continued to ignore, sat in one section, and Angela and I took the furthest seat away from him was being a complete asshole today). I watched them hug each other tightly and my mother blush with excitement about his return. We stood beside them touching each other closely as they made small talk and then we walked over to the baggage claim. I reluctantly remembered the look on my mother's face when I introduced her to Angela.

We parted ways with my folks at the airport and my mother seemed unsettled. I made a mental note to ask her about it when I picked up the dogs in the morning. She mentioned the dogs and Moira getting a hold to one of Dad's shoes. Good! I thought to myself.

"Did you park at the airport?" Angela asked me as her shoulder brushed against mine.

"I did. What about you?"

"No, Katrina dropped me off. She should be here; I gave her the flight information the other day."

"Are you certain? I can drop you off."

"Let me call and see."

I was so caught up in the moment; it only seemed fitting that Angela would ride with me. I put the memory of Katrina way out of my mind. Ever since Angela told me their history and their business arrangement, Katrina was a name I would rather never hear again. I watched Angela turn her back to me and speak quietly with her ex-girlfriend.

Typically not a jealous person, I felt a little uneasy again, and for a moment I thought it was absurd that after our time in Jamaica we were like strangers now. Suddenly, it wasn't known that she and I were working on our own history and could see each other exclusively.

"On second thought," she said as she clicked her phone closed, "I think I will take you up on that offer for a ride home."

"Great. You want to grab something to eat?"

"No, I'd better get home and get back to business; Early day tomorrow."

"Sure. I guess it's just me, since I get to lounge around without a care in the world."

Angela smiled, and we handled airport business and caught the shuttle to my car. She was unusually quiet while I made small talk. I finally opted to say nothing and allowed the smooth sounds of an old Annie

Lennox CD take us to her home.

"I'll call you later," she said after kissing me good-bye and disappearing into her house.

"Later," I replied, trying to avoid the obvious; something was wrong, but until she was ready to talk about it I had to wait. I hit the highway and made it to my side of town in no time. I then slipped inside to rest before my dogs came back home. I was more tired than I thought, and my eyes shut the moment my head hit the pillow on my sofa.

* * *

I slept for what seemed like an eternity until the sound of my home phone woke me from my slumber. "Hello?" I said, half-sleep.

"Hey. You sleeping?"

"I was. What's up?"

"I've got to go out of town."

"Everything OK?"

"Not really. I have to fly out in the morning."

"What is it? Business meeting?"

"I wish it were that simple. I really don't want to talk about it. I just wanted you to know I'd be gone for a couple days."

"OK. Do you know when you'll be back?" I asked as

I sat up and reached for the lamp. With Max and Moira gone and not peeking up from their sleep in need of using the bathroom I noticed the stillness of the house and the quite peace that floated in the air.

"Soon. I mean, I don't know. I'll call you as soon as I know something."

I paused. I didn't want to ask twenty questions. Angela was a businesswoman, and I had to remind myself of such.

"Well, I will let you get back to sleep."

"OK. Call me when you get settled or if you need to talk."

She said bye and hung up. That was awkward. I had to lay back down because going from Jamaica to this was beginning to mess with my head. I forced myself to go to the bathroom then went and laid back on the couch and drifted off to sleep.

* * *

Hours later, at around three in the morning, my phone rang again. "Yeah?" I mumbled.

"Can you meet me at the airport? At five? The plane leaves at six. Some things come up. I need you."

"OK. Which airline?"

"Southwest."

"I'll see you at five."

"OK. And thank you."

"Sure thing. See you in a few."

I got up from the couch and showered quickly. I needed a huge cup of coffee to wake me up. Fixing some, I sent my mother a text, telling her my plans, and asking her to keep the dogs for an additional day or two then I slipped into some jeans and a long sleeve Armani T-shirt. I put on my driving moccasins, grabbed my emergency credit card, and headed to the airport. I put the station on talk radio and listened to the world news. The commentator briefly spoke about the party change back home in Jamaica and the fact that it had been fourteen years and that the new Labor Party should have some sort of positive effect on Jamaica's gloomy economy.

I parked at the gate and met Angela inside. Her eyes were moist and slightly puffy. We left Dallas immediately.

Our flight to Houston Hobby Airport was marked with great silence. Somewhere in my heart, I knew she needed me. Her soft words, which held some sort of guilt, "She's back in Houston. We gotta go get her," was a clear indication of such.

There was sadness and despair in her eyes when I met her at the airport; it was obvious that Katrina had let her down. She had done the unforgivable, and we had better get to her - fast. I knew then that Angela and Katrina shared something powerful and obviously something I would never understand.

Everything was a blur as we boarded the plane, sat quiet quietly and landed shortly thereafter. I observed her mannerisms and purposeful gait she almost glided in her stride as she moved. Still she did not mention why we were here in Houston.

The short flight, our hurried steps, and Angela's firm demeanor were a stark contrast to the warmth of the intense Houston humidity. The luxurious rental we took and the two of us zipping in and out of traffic felt almost as if we were filming a movie. The Jaguar felt more like a Mustang. We pulled into the valet area of *Za Za's* and let the spiked-hair young man take the car to the underground parking lot.

Trailing one step behind Angela, I watched her remain graceful in her stride. Her womanly gait held a power that said, *When this crap is over with and handled, dammit!, I'm going to need a hug!*

The five-star hotel and restaurant were posh and

sophisticated, with pristine floors and modern décor. "Welcome to Za Za's," the soft spoken, mocha-skinned, afro centric young woman said. She smiled with penetrating dimples and fresh pearly whites and spoke in a slight Louisiana dialect.

"My name is Tanisha---How may we help you?"

"A suite if you have it. Nonsmoking." Angela replied with barely enough volume.

"Top floor OK?"

"That's fine."

I turned to survey the hotel and let the two of them conduct business until I heard Angela's voice rise.

"You're kidding, right?"

"No, ma'am; it's been declined."

"This is unbelievable."

"Is everything OK?" I asked and watched as Angela pulled out another credit card.

"We have got to find her. She has access to a lot of money right now, and she can and will fuck it off." Angela said in a tone that meant this was beyond serious.

"Is Visa OK?"

"Yes, we take Visa."

Our transaction complete, Angela was even more rigid now.

"I just need to sit down and think this through. She's probably cashed out the American Express, too. Damn! I knew I should have changed everything over."

I didn't respond. I felt like I was in unknown territory and probably not qualified to respond to something that was between the two of them. The constant buzzing of the elevator as it moved past each floor would have to suffice.

"How could I have been so stupid?" she said aloud with strong conviction in her voice.

She shook her head almost helplessly. Surely, she knew Katrina could or would do something like this. My mother always told me that if you think it, there's probably some truth there. Why else would you get such feelings?

We let ourselves into the exquisite suite, and Angela reached for me and held me tight. "I'm so sorry about this," she said, laying her head on my shoulder.

"It's OK. I'm here as long as you need me."

"This is just so surreal."

"We'll get through it. I promise."

"I've got to shower and lie down. No telling where she is now, but, come night, I know exactly where to find her."

"Come, let's get you showered and let you get some rest."

I helped her get set for her shower and set out some towels and something for her to sleep in. While she showered, I set the bed for her and programmed my iPod for relaxing selections so she could drift off, hopefully with no worries. Thankfully, she did.

I watched her sleep for a few hours, then went down to the bar area to call my mother.

"Mom?"

"Hi, sweetie."

"Mom, I'm in Houston with Angela. You got the text right? She and her business partner are having some issues. I should be home sometime tomorrow."

"Everything OK?"

"I'm not sure. Angela is pretty upset. She's sleeping now."

"Sounds serious. Is the business partner in any trouble?"

"Mom, I'm not sure. She says some things that lead me to believe that this partner is a little shady, or has a shady past."

"And is this partner in any way involved in your contract, and what you're trying to do?"

"I didn't ask. I probably should have, but I don't want to be selfish right now. This is about Angela; not my selling potential."

"OK, but that is something to think about. You've worked too hard, Claude, to get caught up in some sort of scheme."

"I don't think it's a scheme. Angela is a businesswoman. What's happening with her partner has nothing to do with me."

"OK, if that's what you say. Now tell me, how was your trip back home?"

"Awful until Angela joined me."

"Yeah, I saw that. Did you invite her?"

"Kind of, but, nonetheless, it was great having her there." I paused, then continued, "Mom, Father showed me another side of him. It was surprising and disappointing."

"Claude, your father is under a great deal of stress, trying to handle your uncle's affairs."

"Well, you couldn't tell. He acted as if he wanted nothing to do with Uncle Peter. Why did he even show up?"

"No one else would do it."

"Are you serious?"

"I'm afraid so. You see, your Uncle Peter was or is considered to be an outcast there; no one wants to associate themselves with him right now."

"But he's family, and a well known cricket player there. What's changed?"

"And he's also homosexual, and in Jamaica that is forbidden."

"What? Nonsense, Mom. No way."

"It's true. Uncle Peter was badly beaten a couple months ago because someone linked him to that lifestyle. It was at that time that it was discovered that he was positive or in fact had AIDS."

"Mom, I knew nothing of this. You and Dad said nothing except that he was sick."

"We didn't want you to worry."

"But what about who I am? I could have helped him get some agencies involved to help."

"And that's what your father did not want."

Click. I was a lost for words and like a knee jerk reaction I hung up the phone and stared at the receiver. I began to think.

My so-called loving and supportive father was a liar. It was OK to be gay as long as I was here in the states and out of the way. Not to mention, his absurd antics while I was there; he was so harsh. It was like I was in the way. My heart sank. So much for believing all these years that my parents were supportive of who I am.

My cell phone vibrated in my hand. I looked at the screen, which blinked 'Pops.' I had half a mind not to answer, but part of me wanted to know why he had lied to me all these years.

"Hello?"

"Claude?"

"Yes, Father."

"Me no wan you to be angry wit me. Me pickney important."

"Pops, this is just too much. I can't talk about it now."

"Me pickney dem. Me have two bwoys ....me no worry about yuh and weh ya do." His words were fading in or out or I was becoming light headed

"What did you just say? Who are your children? What sons are you talking about? Am I not' your only child?"

"What is going on? Where's Mom? Does she know?" I asked as my heart began to beat a mile a minute.

"DOES SHE KNOW?" I yelled through the phone.

"No," he said softly almost ashamed. There was a long pause. He mentioned something about Mom being in the shower when clarity kicked in then went on to say what sounded like curse words, insults and plain ole fashion hurt.

"Yuh Me tird daughter. You av two bredda five years younger an you."

"What are you talking about, Pops? What does Mom say about this? And does she even know?" I really didn't want to hear is trite answers right now but my mouth kept asking questions. I had to get off the phone before I said something that I would regret so I decided to end the call.

"Pops, do we have to do this now? This is not something we can just talk about over the phone. This isn't politics or a conversation about the damn Yankees!"

"Yes, Claude. Now. Me wan tell you for soooo long. So long, bebee. Me sorry ef me urt you gal in Jamaica. Me no wan you involved in those politics. Uncle Peter, sodomite bwoy ef me say too much, yuh be exposed."

Click.

I had heard enough. Both my parents had been lying to me either directly or indirectly all my life. Hell, I could be adopted for all I know. I shoved my phone deep into my pockets and headed to the elevators. I felt like my entire body was moving in slow motion. How could this be?

-Ten-

Around 11 o'clock or so that night, Angela and I took to the streets of Houston. We both were quiet and silently battling something deep inside. For her, probably money for me, my entire life being a sham.

After making our way from highways to back streets to some old shopping center, we parked and walked towards a club. Its patrons, all dressed in flashy clothes and wild hairstyles, were loud as they talked about God-knows-what, sounding like little birds chirping. After joining the line outside, we moved along in the slow procession until we made it to the cashier, where a boney guy with a metal detector and an over-aged security guard stood in the corner, watching us.

"Ten dollars," the Mohawk, gold-toothed, busty woman said.

"I'm here for Katrina. Is she here tonight?"

"Yeah, she here."

Just as Angela began to speak, the woman recognized her and said, "My bad A; go 'head. She should be in the back."

"She's with me," Angela calmly said as I smiled at the woman, then followed Angela to what seemed to be

the pit of hell! The club was dark and smoky, the concrete floors seemed moist against my Clarks, and, if the music weren't so loud, surely I would have heard hear them peeling from the floor each time I took a step.

The bar sat in the middle of two areas, each playing two types of music: one, traditional R&B and Hip Hop; the other, Dirty South. I felt like a kitten in the midst of ten thousand angry dogs. The people were rough, hazy, and incoherent, almost as though there were something in the music or punch that had them in a trance. I was uncomfortable, to say the least.

We stopped at the bar, ordered bottled water, then waited for Katrina to make an appearance. The whole scene played out like an awful movie as women in G-strings and damn near everything else flapped around, shaking their asses to everything. Broke-down heels, mismatched outfits, and bad weaves and a *Black and Mild* cigar seemed to be the night's special. I watched them prance and drop, then rub themselves against one another. The way they performed was almost ceremonial; I wanted to puke!

I suddenly realized that Angela had left my side. After surveying the sidewalls, which were layered with chairs, I found her towards the end, standing nose-to-nose with someone I hoped was Katrina. She was a slender stud, tall with shaven hair and milk chocolate dreamy skin. Baggin'-and-saggin' with a nice button-down on, she seemed to ignore Angela as she talked with her hands, pointing them at her head. I turned away; I didn't want to seem nosy.

My heart was beating a mile a minute. I had not come there to fight my way out. I was glad that I opted for fatigue pants, a muscle-T, and my Clarks, with my locks up in a ponytail. I clearly stood out from this crowd - and with one false move, my ass was toast!

I turned around to check on them again, and they were gone. I then moved to the edge of a wall, positioned myself for comfort (and a quick way out, if need be), placed my cell back on vibrate, and continued to watch the entertainment – or, should I say, lack thereof. It was damn near two in the morning when I felt someone stand beside me.

"Hey, you," she leaned in and whispered. "I'm sorry about that. This is taking longer than I realized." In such a chaotic environment, her smooth tone seemed insane, but the hint of cognac that danced around my ear and face said she'd had a drink or two.

"Last call. Do you need anything?"

"I'm good," I said, trying to hide my disgust. What the hell was this? Some sort of joke? I stood up from the wall, pushed Angela away, and was headed out of there when the lights flickered, and like ants at a picnic, people grabbed chairs and brought them around the dance floor.

"I'm really sorry," she said as a drag queen in all the wrong colors yelled, "Are ya'll ready for the show?"

"YEAH!" everyone yelled back.
I said to Angela, "Are you kidding? It's almost two - what show?"

"She's coming; she just has to talk to the crowd." I shook my head, this time not hiding my disgust. She really meant that we were going to *get* Katrina - *literally!* I stood away from her and waited another half hour before Katrina - or *K-Rock,* as they called her - took the stage. With shades on and a drink in her hand, she thanked everyone for coming out and supporting her club; it was *her* club.

She lifted her shades and rubbed her bloodshot eyes, and it was quickly evident that she was high as a kite. She rubbed her chin and sucked her top teeth in-between words - and immediately I knew what was going on: she was a drug user. I had had enough and turned to walk out when Angela grabbed me.

"It's not what you think."

"Look, I've been here all night, and it's time to go. You do what you have to. I can catch a cab."

"A cab? You find a cab here tonight, and I'll be surprised."

I looked at her. She was drunk; clearly not the woman that I saw at the club, who read my poetry or who gracefully put on an event with thousands of high-class lesbians only weeks ago.

"Here, take the keys. I have to drive Katrina anyway."

I grabbed the keys and made my way to the exit, knowing that I left Angela there staring at the back of my head. I managed to find the car, the freeway, and the hotel without screaming at the top of my lungs, "LAWD AV MERCY!" This here was some bull crap. I had half a mind to drive myself to the airport and let those two figure out what the hell to do.

When I arrived at the hotel, I nodded at the dimple-faced chick from earlier and made my way to the room. I went straight to the shower and rinsed off all the dirt and grime that seemed to be all over me. I couldn't even think about Angela and her ragamuffin ex-girlfriend. I had seen enough; Katrina was a *Lego beast* in every sense of the word!

I scrubbed myself with an intensity that screamed, "MERCY!" My hair, toes, hands, and everything else I could think of took a beat down. Finally, after brushing my teeth for ten minutes, I wrapped myself in a T-shirt and towel and fell into a deep sleep.

-Eleven-

I woke up to a soft stroke against my hand. She twirled it some, letting her hand glide up and down my index finger. I opened my eyes as she handed me a glass of water.

"Hey."

"Thought you could use some water."

"Thank you," I said, and took a drink.

"You want to talk?"

"Sure," I said and sat up from the bed, letting my head, rest against the headboard. She sat on the bed and touched my forearm. The hotel room offered no comfort, even though it was a top-of-the-line room with all the makeup of high scale and high class. The images of the club and how Angela carried herself were etched in my brain, and the truth was, the woman I had thought I had fallen in love with was simply nowhere to be found.

"I'm really sorry about this. Katrina is having a hard time right now, and I honestly don't know what to do. "

"Where is she?"

"On the couch, passed out."

I turned away. I wasn't ready to hear what I suspected or thought would take place.

"I can't leave her like this, Claude. It's just not right."

"So, what are you saying?"

Angela sighed deeply. "This isn't easy for me, Claude. You know it isn't."

"Angela, apparently I don't know anything."

"Wait; listen, we still have business to conduct. I just think we need to focus on that and not get involved."

"I agree. And, to be honest, let me rethink the business part," I said, looking deep into her eyes in the barely lit room.

"But we have a deal."

"Angela, I'm serious. I just think all of this is weird. You meet me down in Jamaica for four days, screw my brains out, and we do damn near everything together except say the words 'I love you' - and now this?"

"Please. This isn't easy for me. I care about you so much. You know I do."

"You're not hearing me. This does not make sense to me. So, either you tell me what's going on, or you will never see me again. And I mean that."

"You're giving me an ultimatum?"

"No, I'm asking you to tell me what's really going on because this isn't making sense. You two are business partners - what does that have to do with me? You're telling me that, since she is in a crisis, you no longer feel anything for me? That makes absolutely no sense, so talk to me."

"It's complicated."

"I'm listening."

"Claude, please, not right now."

I gently touched the side of her face, then turned it to look directly at me and said, "It has to be now."

Sighing, she stood and shut the door; surely, what we shared had to overcome this.

"You really are going to make me do this?" she said.

I shook my head, indicating "Yes."

"I don't want to hurt you, Claude."

"Just tell me what's going on."

She sat beside me and put her feet on the bed. Moving closer to me, she laid her head on my shoulders, then said, "Katrina is - or was - in recovery. She's had a hard life, and when we were together almost four years ago she was completely clean - completely. I met her through some friends, and she was so sweet. At the time, she was everything I wanted."

"How long were you two together?"

"Six years."

"That's a very long time. You didn't say all of this when we were in Jamaica."

"I know. I told you it was complicated. I feel like I've lied to you. It wasn't intentional. A huge part of me wants to forget all about what Katrina and I had. Those six years together were hard. She struggled on and off, and I was there each time to pick up the pieces.

"She's the last girlfriend I had. I literally lived and breathed her. We've lived here in Houston, Dallas, in California, and in Atlanta. I helped her start her club, and she helped me with my agency. We are each other's silent partners. Up until the start of this year, I told her that we needed to have our own thing and see how it worked. She still accompanies me to many of my functions, and we haven't technically parted ways in the manner of business. It's so much and so complicated. But she's never done anything like this - cashing out our credit cards and business accounts."

"Is that where the Taylor in the business name

comes from?"

"No."

"Do you still love her?"

"I will always love her."

"Are you still in love with her?"

"No, I'm not."

"So what's the problem? Why can't you break away from her?"

"I told you it's complicated."

"NO, what you've told me is that you are no longer in love with her, that you two helped each other with business ventures, and that she is in recovery."

"She was in recovery."

"She's using again?"

"Yes," she said softly, and I noticed that she was crying; her teardrops hit my T-shirt.

"It isn't your fault, Angela."

"It is. She's been wanting to get back together, and I've told her that I wasn't ready for a relationship again. I wanted to work on my business. She saw the way I looked at you when we were at Tryst, then Jamaica...she's having a hard time dealing with it."

"That still doesn't make it your fault. She has a mind of her own. She's also grown."

'There's something else, Claude," she said, pressing deep into me and holding me tight. "She's positive."

"Positive about what?"

"HIV-positive."

My heart stopped and my body fell limp as Angela held me close, crying what felt like a waterfall of tears. This was not happening to me; I refused to accept the fact that sitting so close to me was the virus, staring me dead in my face. I didn't close my eyes the rest of the night; I just held her as those words danced around in my head, *'HIV-POSITIVE.'*

I couldn't even fathom if it affected me or this woman who I clearly loved, who loved me as she mourned for me, for her, and for Katrina. A love like that, you can't help but appreciate.

Yet, those words still danced, harshly taunting, *'HIV-POSITIVE.'* When the sun peeked over my shoulder, and my eyes had found no sleep, I found myself wondering. How long had she known or suspected this? And when in the hell was she going to tell me?!

-Twelve-

It had been more than a month since I'd slipped away from Angela's embrace in the early morning hours. Quietly, I had packed my belongings, caught a taxi to the airport, and got on a Southwest flight headed home. There was something about the way she told me that pushed me away from her; I felt like she was holding something else back, and that scared me more than anything.

She emailed pertinent information to me regarding the publication of my book, set me up with one of their editors to finalize everything, and texted information to me about events that I should attend. We said nothing of our conversation, though; it was business, and that was it. Faking sick, I declined a Labor Day event, and I eventually drifted back into depression as the Fall decided to rear its head around mid-September. My daily routine was to get up, take my medication, and drink some green tea while my dogs played in the back yard, and then climb back into bed.

As I lay in bed, I thought about Uncle Peter, the lies my family told me, and how who I was fit into all of it. I was shunned in Jamaica and didn't even know it. My father had kept my life a complete secret, but I guess a woman with a tight ass and enough breasts kept suspicion to a minimum.

I never felt I had to hide it. I never brought any men with me when I came home, and, although I never spoke of any of my relationships to anyone, I thought they all surely knew. Maybe it was the twist in my hips, my sparkling green eyes, or my soft mulatto skin and womanly features.

I had to find out why there were so many lies - and who exactly was this other family I had? Two younger brothers and two older sisters? Did they have the same mother? My father was a hypocrite, sitting back in the states with secrets tucked away in Jamaica.

It was times like this when I needed my mother, whose strength, wisdom, and answers would, no doubt, not be pretty at all. I couldn't help realizing, though, that she had lied, too.

The ringing of the house phone snapped me out of my twisted thoughts. I ignored it, but then I remembered that I hadn't turned the volume down on the answering machine after I'd listened to one of the eight messages before erasing them all.

"Ms. Moore, this is Gillian. I was calling about our editing session. If you could, give me a call at 214-555-7287. See you soon. Bye."

There wasn't a snowball's chance in hell that I was going to call her back. In fact, I wasn't in the mood for anything related to my craft. I got up to turn the answering machine off when the phone rung again. Immediately, the machine clicked on, which indicated that I had more messages to check.

"Actually," Gillian's bubbly voice said, "I will come to you this evening, say around five or so - traffic permitting. Okay. See you then."

I knew that was Angela's doing. Gillian had no idea where I lived, how to get there, or if she were even welcome. I guess signing that contract with Angela's agency meant I had a fucking obligation to get this editing done, whether I felt like it or not.

Bitch. She had some nerve to be thinking about her agency and herself. But, I guess she figured that since I'd slipped away that morning and left her to deal with Katrina, it was all I could give her.

Reluctantly, I bathed and slipped into some sweats and a long sleeve T-shirt. I gathered all of my work and what she needed to review, then set my office up for our session. It was a little after six when my doorbell rang.

"Good evening, Ms. Moore," the smooth-skinned, doe-eyed girl said. I quickly realized that it was the bartender from Angela's event. "I moonlight from time to time," she said with a wink.

"How are you? Come on in."

"This is nice. Did you do all of this yourself?"

"I did, thank you. Follow me; my office is just down the way."

We nestled into my office and went over my proposed manuscript, then she showed me her suggestions. They weren't too bad and didn't take away my voice or lose sight of what I was trying to accomplish.

After we finished, we sat outside, sipping on Jamaican Blue Mountain coffee and conversing about everything from the troops coming home to lifestyles to family and growing up as an only child. She told me her friends called her "Gill" and that I should do the same. I told her she could drop the "Ms. Moore" and just call me "Claude."

"'Claude,' huh?"

"Yeah, like Jean 'Claude' Van Damme."

"The actor, right?"

"Exactly."

"He's old school; I love watching his old movies. I know I don't look a day over 25, but I like to see myself as a 40-year-old chic type of woman. And besides, my son would die if I wasn't 'so cool' - as he states."

"That's right. You did say you had a son. Fourteen?"

"Correct. What about you? Any children, or hopes of having one?"

"I don't know. I'm getting pretty up there in age now. It's probably too late, though."

"It isn't too late; you just need to find the right person and settle down."

I smiled, trying to hide the pain of missing Angela. I wanted to blurt out all of my sorrows and cry on someone's shoulder - but it wasn't going to be Gillian's.

"Penny for your thoughts?"

I shook my head. "It's nothing."

"You sure? Seemed liked you drifted away for a second."

"I did. I'm sorry."

"One of those days, huh?"

"I suppose," I said with a heavy sigh that came from the depths of my soul. I was missing Angela so much, I could barely stand to talk to Gillian. I wanted to know what she was doing or if she was still with Katrina - and why in the hell hadn't she come to see me and tell me this was all some sort of mix up?

"You're drifting again," Gillian said in a soft voice.

"Sorry," I said with a slight grin.

She smiled back. "We need to get you out of this house, Claude; that's what you need. Come on, let's go to the mixer tonight. You could really use it."

"No, I think I'm going to stay in tonight." *And the rest of any other night,* I wanted to add.

"You can't do that. That's unreasonable and no way for a beautiful young artist to live. Now, as your editor, I command you to get your sexy self dressed and accompany me to this event."

"Gillian, how about we just focus on work for right now? That is why you are here, right?"

"I was, but you zoning in and out is tripping me out. No wonder you're experiencing writer's block! Something's got a hold of you, and that's all you can focus on. Come on, you want to make Oprah, right?"

"Oprah? Where does she come in?"

"Oh, please, that's every writer's dream: to sit on that fabulous leather sofa and talk about their book and how and when it all started and the inspiration.

Puhleeze! Try that on someone else."

"Real cute, Gillian. What time does it start?"

"It started an hour ago."

"Somehow I knew you were going to say that. What about we go to the next one?'

"There's no better time than the present."

I really felt no need to get out so soon after Angela had dropped the "H-Bomb" on me. My anxiety level was sky high. At times, I wanted to run to the doctor's or home to my folks, but for some reason I felt comfort in my new pastime of puffing cigarettes and laying in bed, flipping through channels. Max, Moira, and I were on a routine: get up, go outside, pour a glass of wine, green tea or coffee, and climb back in bed and pretend like I was watching television.

"OK, but I have to shower first." I lied. I was trying to stall so she would change her mind.

"Yes, that would be wise."

"Actually, I bathed earlier...who cares, anyway? I'm going just like this."

"Ahhhh, Claude...it is a business function with some pretty sophisticated women there – who may just be potential buyers of your book. You probably want to re-think that, huh?"

"Right; I forgot about that. See, that's why I need to catch the next one."

"No, that's why you need to go. Your new book will be out soon. You have got to get yourself out there, and now would be best."

"Agreed. Let me jump into something a bit more appropriate. I'll be right back."

-Thirteen-

The ride in Gillian's rugged Jeep had my stomach all over the place by the time we pulled up to the club, called MINC. Fall was definitely upon us, and I was grateful that I wore a blazer with my jeans and boots. Gillian talked mostly about her son, Josh, and I listened, hoping that Angela would be anywhere but here tonight.

Just shy of eight o'clock, we made our way into the bountiful abundance of beautiful women in their professional or chic attire. We headed straight to the bar. Gillian motioned to the bartender, and he brought us two of whatever Gillian always ordered. In two gulps, I was done and looking to the bartender to fix me another. Two more gulps, and I was done again. I then turned to survey the crowd - when I noticed Angela and Katrina in an embrace that made my stomach turn and my limbs feel weak. My eyes were fixed on them as they laughed in each other's arms, sharing a closeness that was unspeakable.

"You okay?" Gillian asked, snapping me out of my haze.

"Oh, yeah; I'm fine." I'd lied, of course. She then looked in the direction that I had been staring in and looked back at me.

"There's the Dynamic Duo," she said, sounding slightly sarcastic.

"Is that what they call it these days?"

"Yeah, those two have been together for years and have been called just about everything."

"I thought Angela was from California?"

"No, she and Katrina moved to California, then to Atlanta and Houston, but they are both from here."

"Didn't know that. So, what else is there to know about the *Dynamic Duo*?"

"Nothing, except that they're joined at the hip, inseparable, and madly in love. They're each other's only family. You know how it is in the gay community."

"Actually, no, I don't. I have both my parents, and a host of relatives that support me and whom I can lean on."

"Really?"

"You don't?"

"Well, it's complicated. I was once married and so coming out to my folks was a bit tough but I'm headstrong. My folks, knew that they would lose both me and Josh if they pushed the issue about my life and who I was. A lesbian. So I guess in default I managed to keep the support of my family but you know plenty of lesbians don't have that. They have make shift families, which usually consist of friends and exes. But I'm sure you know that already."

"I guess I never looked at it like that. I never had to count on friends for family because the three of us, my parents and I, have been so close."

"Well consider yourself lucky. Katrina and Angela are outcasts in their families, plus they have this connection that keeps them inseparable. It's almost tragic the love they share."

"Really? I thought they were broken up?" I said, trying my best to hide my jealousy and vulnerability; so much of me wanted to sprint over to Angela - leaving a trail of turned over lesbians and drinks behind me - and ask her how long she had known about Katrina's status; how dare she drag me into the debacle of their so-called way of doing things? Their distorted kind of "love" ruins lives.

"You want to go to the patio?"

"Sure. There's nothing in here worth looking at."

I followed Gillian through the crowd of women, bypassing Angela and Katrina, who obviously noticed me because I felt Katrina's eyes following me. We slipped into the darkness of old palm-like trees, dimly lit street lamps, and the stench of Marlboro cigarettes. The patio was scarcely occupied, and we made our way to a rustic table in the corner and sat and talked.

Gillian had one of her bartender friends bring us out some drinks, and we sat and talked about my book and my writer's block, which seemed to have me in a chokehold of sorts.

"Claude, what about personal things that you may be dealing with? Can't you write about that?"

"You mean losing my job and falling in love with a woman that's already taken? No thanks."

"Falling in love, huh? You mind if I ask with whom?"

"It's not even important. In fact, I'd rather talk about the jerks at the newspaper than about her."

"Must have been serious...did she feel the same way?"

"I guess not."

"Now, that's tough to deal with. Are you going to be okay?"

"Do I have a choice? Besides, it's complicated anyway. I wouldn't even know where to start," I said, then looked up to see Katrina walking towards me with a look on her face that let me know she had a thing or two to say to me.

"Can I speak to you for a second?" she said in a grim tone.

"Hey, Katrina," Gillian interjected.

"Hey, wassup, Gill. Can you excuse us for a second?"

Gillian stood, looked at me, and said, "You OK?"

"Sure. I'll be in--- in a sec."

I stood and faced Katrina, looking into her deep dark eyes, which had a hint of yellow that should have been white. She probably was not only HIV positive, but also had Hepatitis A, B, and C!

"What can I do for you?"

"Well, for starters you can leave Angela alone. We're back together."

"I don't know what you are talking about. Angela and I have a business deal. Is that what you are referring to?"

"WE have a business deal. Anything she does, I'm a part of it."

"And how does that bother you? Seems like, between the three of us, there is some money to be made, and basically it's money over bullshit."

"I don't like you. No, I really don't like you. Ever since she inked that deal, I have been trying to find ways to destroy you."

"'Destroy?' That's a heavy word, don't you think? More importantly, is it that serious?" This seemed surreal talking to this low class individual. I found myself listening hard to her lack of grammar or looking at all the imperfections in her face asking myself what does Angela see in this girl?

"I will slap the shit out of you. You don't know me."

"Nor do I care to," I said, folding my arms across my chest and staring back at her in her all black outfit and pointed toe boots. She looked like some sort of desperado or thug from a movie.

"Bitchah," she said, clinching her teeth like the gangster I knew she was, "I will destroy you."

"Hey, you two," Angela called out. She had on a matching black outfit, only with a fitted woman's blazer - not the leather vest that Katrina sported; she was oblivious to this gangster and her antics. Perhaps.

We both looked at her as if to say, You better get your friend.

I started to walk off and passed Angela when she

touched my side and said, "Hey, how are you? Glad you made it out." She then looked at Katrina. "You two getting acquainted, I see. That's good. We want to take care of our clients."

While Angela stared at me, Katrina squinted her eyes, then looked at me and mouthed surreptitiously, "Destroy you."

I walked off and left the two of them talking, then found my way back to Gillian, who was in the midst of a couple of exotic women. They were tall, slender, and absolutely gorgeous. I stood beside them and listened as they talked about a planned trip to Belize that summer. The bartender found us and brought drinks for them, then took my order: Martini straight, not chilled, no fruit, no olive or toothpick -just straight!

I tried to calm down about Katrina and her silly antics, as well as the fact that Angela actually thought the three of us could work under those circumstances. I was wondering who was going to say something first about Katrina being HIV-positive and the fact that Angela and I had slept together on more than one occasion?

I felt the steam roll off my skin as I waited for the drink that I ordered; I stood there, trying not to rain on her parade. All I could think about was why in the world

- better yet, what in the world would possess Angela to stand there like nothing was wrong? And that psycho, Katrina, threatening me! I wanted so much to call my mother; I knew we could have a candid talk about this and that she would offer some sort of insight that would make everything a little easier to deal with; after all, there was no mild way of dealing with the fact that I, too, might be HIV-positive, and just the thought of that was killing me softly. I had had so many crazy dreams since our conversation, and I was sleeping on the sofa with the television on, sausage'd in-between Max and Moira, who seemed to know that their mama was going to die soon…real soon.

My eyes became moist, and I couldn't believe that I was actually choked up in the middle of all these women. I was angry at this lifestyle that had more drama than I cared to deal with. Everyone was linked in some way and there never seemed to be the possibility that you could find true love.

"Here, this one is on the house," Angela said, grabbing my free hand. We walked hand-in–hand toward the front door, her leading me outside as I gulped down a shot of Patron and put the glass on a nearby table. I was beginning to wonder just who was the possessed one because, as she led, I followed with no argument or struggle.

As the cool Fall air hit my skin, I yanked away from her, asking, "Where's your girl?" I was as green as green could be, so consumed with jealousy that I felt like a kid at a schoolyard fight. Mad; mad because Angela took so long to find me and cater to my deflated ego.

"What girl?" she asked, folding her arms across her chest.

"Oh, please; I saw you two together when I walked in. Don't play dumb with me - it isn't very becoming. And what are we out here for?"

"I've been meaning to call you."

"Right. I can't tell; you all hugged up with Katrina. I guess you've had your hands full, right? With all of her issues - which is strange; seems like I should be in this loop, too, don't you think?"

"It isn't what you think, Claude."

"Don't tell me what I think. You have no idea what I have been dealing with. You're just interested in selling books."

"That's not fair. We need to talk, Claude."

"No, we don't. The last time you said that, it wasn't anything I wanted to hear."

"You're here with Gill. Does that mean you are finishing up the book?"

"Look, I think we need to rethink this book. I can't write these days. My mind is preoccupied."

"Claude, we have a contract and a deadline; it isn't that simple."

"Simple? You have got to be kidding me, right? Do you even know what I have been dealing with since I last saw you? Do you even remember the last conversation we had? You know what - just forget it. Forget it. I don't ever want to see or hear from you again, so figure out a way to make this go away."

I walked off, pulling my arm away as she tried to stop me. I went inside and ran directly into Gillian, who was with the bartender that took my order. I grabbed the drink gulped it down then turned back around. She followed me to her Jeep, unlocked it, and we jumped back in and sped off with Angela watching and Katrina standing beside her.

I was angry at myself--- I had already signed the damn contract!

-Fourteen-

After waking up drenched from a nightmare that I couldn't remember, I slipped on my flip-flops and went to my office. My head felt like a roller coaster was running over it, and the more I tried to move forward, the more it hurt. I was going to Angela, and she had better tell me something. I flipped on the light to my office and saw Gillian asleep on my sofa; I had forgotten that she had stayed over because Josh was with his dad and we had had a little too much to drink earlier.

"Hey," she said as I sat at my desk. She rubbed her eyes and shook off the sleep.

"Hey, Gillian. Sorry to wake you. I just need to find something really quick."

"Anything I can help with?" She asked politely as she sat up.

"Actually," I said, looking around my screen, "I need to know where to find Angela."

"Her office or home?"

"Either."

"Well, she's probably home, considering the time. She's in North Dallas, off Preston. I can show you."

"Can you take me now? I've been there once but

can't remember for the life of me how to get there."

"Sure, but it's one in the morning; can we do it tomorrow?"

"It has to be now."

"OK…is everything okay?"

"I need to deal with this business crap. I'm not doing business with some crook or gangster."

"Angela?"

"Her or that Katrina. Do you know she threatened me tonight? I'm not making a penny for either one of those wenches!

"Last night? At the mixer?"

"Yeah. When you left us outside, she had the nerve to tell me that she's been wanting to destroy me ever since I made that deal with Angela."

"Are you serious?"

"As a heart attack."

"Does Angela know this? Surely, she wouldn't allow this."

"Gillian, I don't know what she knows. One day, she's this way, then it's like we are complete strangers."

"Well, you know, some have said that Katrina turned her out."

"Out like how?" I asked furiously, knowing this story was probably going to get worse.

"Well, Angela comes from uppity folk. Her parents are well-to-do, successful doctors or lawyers - or one is a doctor and one is a lawyer – but ever since she hooked up with Katrina she's been going down. Personally, she's been the same with me. We went to the same high school, and College, and she's the same classy, overly dressed 'pretty girl' that everyone wants to date."

Typical in this lifestyle; The pretty, classy ones going for the bad guy just like in Heterosexual relationships. What is it with women that think they can change the bad guy!

"But how does that make her turned out?"

"Her parents have disowned her. I told you they are considered outcast. I've also heard rumors of her being a cokehead or that she used to be a cokehead. But, like I said, she's the same with me. We've worked together in the literary capacity for awhile now."

"So, how did you start working for her?"

"Well, we used to work together on our high school newspaper. We both went to SMU and did our journalism and creative writing things there and just kept in touch. After we graduated, she saw me, I think, at a poetry club years ago. She told me about her agency and wanted to know if I would come on as her editor and partner. I did."

"You're the Taylor? In Murphy & Taylor?" My mouth dropped as soon as those words left my mouth.

"Gillian Marie Taylor---Yes, that's me."

"I didn't know." I let out a snicker because I had been running my mouth and all along, Gill was a part of their team. I began to shake my head.

"I handle the editing and own about forty percent of the company those two have the other sixty." She said and shrugged her shoulders to indicate that perhaps it was just business and nothing personal.

"Is she trustworthy?"

"She has been, as far as I know. Now, Katrina - that's something I know very little about. I can only say that she seems a little beneath Angela, and for the life of me I don't know why she would date someone with such a harsh and rugged past."

"Why then would you go into business with them?"

"Well the way Angela explained it, was Katrina was there as a silent partner but all the money that was put up was all hers from a trust fund. But trust I had my ex-husbands cousin, who's an entertainment lawyer check it out. Julian said it was legit. And I know my cousin, he wouldn't steer me wrong."

"If you say so. They just seem crooked."

"I think substance abuse might be an issue but that's them."

" So that brings some validity to the whole 'turning Angela out' theory?"

"Right. Because Katrina was a dealer when they met; everyone knew that. And, I thought, *why would she hook up with a drug dealer?* It just didn't make since; whatever went down, though, Angela never let it show. She's just a classy woman."

"So, does she still deal?"

"Oh, no. The business they conduct is all legit because I would not be a part of it if it were anything else. I have a son to look out for; I don't have time for mess like that. They use, but don't deal."

"So, you were a teen mother?" I asked changing the subject. It was obvious I had a lot to learn about the surface or the front that people put up. I would have never thought Angela had a drug problem.

"No, silly. I'm forty, and my son is fourteen - which would mean I had him when I was twenty six."

I stared at Gill she was a beautiful strong black

woman. She was the natural girl that was simply beautiful. Everything about her was beautiful. She said the right words at the right time, the way her locs fell back neatly into place and the way she talked about her son and being a mother. I don't ever recall hearing one nasty, cuss or impolite word leaving her mouth.

"You're right. I'm sorry; you just look so young and vibrant."

"Good genes, sweetie, good genes."

"OK let's do this before I lose my nerve." And before my head exploded I wanted to say---it was killing me!

"Break the business deal, right?" Gillian asked with a smirk that made it seem as if she could read my mind. She probably knew thanks to Angela that it all had very little to do with business; she just didn't say anything.

"Right. Break the business deal. Come on."

"Are you going to change?"

"No, I'm going like this. The more time I waste, the less I'll be willing to do this."

"Maybe you should re-think it and go by there tomorrow?"

"No, it has to be now," I said, then vanished into the kitchen, grabbed two Aleve and popped them in my mouth like Tic Tacs, swallowing them without water.

With no more words, we set off to North Dallas, veering off 635 West, making a right off Preston, and taking a side road through an upscale neighborhood until we found Angela's home. It was a beautiful, modest one-story with fine greenery on full display, even during that time of the year. We parked in front and sat for a moment as Gillian shut off the motor. The temperature was cool, but my insides kept me warm. I couldn't put together any pieces or show any concern or worry if Katrina answered the door. I needed to know about this 'positive status' that was looming over me and holding me hostage.

"You have your phone?"

I took her phone and punched in Angela's number. After the third ring, someone picked up.

"Hello?" the soft voice said. I paused, trying to figure out if it were Angela or Katrina.

"Hello?" she said again, as if she were trying to sit up and listen closely to hear anything.

"Angela?"

"Yes, this is Angela." I heard her moving, like she was getting out of the bed.

"Where you going?" Katrina asked in the background.

"Go back to sleep, hon. It's a business call."

Katrina must have rolled back over. Angela made soft steps as she moved to a private area. I waited, trying to find the right words to say. She shut a door behind her.

"Claude?"

"I need to talk to you."

"Where are you?"

"Outside."

"Here?"

"Yes. Are you coming out?"

"Yes. Let me grab my robe."

Click. I hung up, let myself out of the jeep, leaned against it, and slipped my hands in my pockets. I felt my eyes getting moist and looked down at my chilled toes in my leather-strapped flip-flops. After a couple minutes, Angela emerged and walked over to me in her long, pink terrycloth robe.

"Hey," she said as she leaned against the jeep beside me. I heard Gill turn up her radio in the jeep to give us some privacy.

"Hey," I said, almost inaudible.

"You OK?"

"Not really."

"It's chilly out here. You want to come inside?"

I looked at her like she had lost her mind.

"Ahhh, no...that would be a little odd, don't you think?"

"Katrina's sleeping."

"What's going on?" I asked her though I wasn't sure I wanted to hear her response.

"What do you mean?"

"What do I mean? Are you serious? Or have you conveniently forgotten our Houston trip, our Jamaican vacation, or what transpired between us?"

"I haven't forgotten anything," she said, looking down at her matching slippers. "It's complicated, Claude. Very complicated."

"Complicated? That's all you have to say?"

"Well, what do you want me to say? That's all I can say."

"What?" I stood up from the Jeep because I couldn't believe what I was hearing. After all I'd said to her, she was still giving me some bull crap about it being complicated.

"What about your status and Katrina being positive?"

"It's a private issue, Claude. Very private."

"Private? This crap isn't private! WE, YOU ME -"

"Lower your voice, Claude, please; we have neighbors."

"'We have neighbors???' I don't give a damn about your neighbors!"

"Walk with me."

"No! I want answers."

"Walk with me, Claude." She stood up from the Jeep and walked away from her home. I followed her. She stopped underneath a huge oak tree, folded her arms across her chest, and looked at me.

"I love her. I will not leave her like this. We've been together through thick and thin. It's not right to leave like this. And I know," she said as her voice became heavy, "I was wrong to let things go down like they did with us. I'm sorry if I hurt you. I never intended to hurt you."

Staring at her, I was at a loss for words. I felt like I was the butt of some sick joke: I had lost my job, had been used by Angela, and had possibly become infected with HIV - all in such a short time period. My heart ached, and my soul felt like it left my body. How in the world did I let this happen?

"I guess it didn't mean to you what it meant to me.

I guess all of this was just some game to you, huh?"

"No, it wasn't a game."

"Then what the hell would you call it? I never asked for any of this. You initiated everything, and now you want me to act like nothing occurred and that the big ass pink elephant by the name of 'HIV' or the 'VIRUS' or 'THE MONSTER' doesn't exist? What the hell is wrong with you? Huh? What is wrong with you? Are you schizophrenic or something? Bipolar? A sociopath, maybe? WHAT?!!" I yelled.

"I'm not sure if I'm positive. Katrina is, though, and I would appreciate it if you would stop throwing it around like it's some joke or something. This doesn't concern you."

I wanted to wrap my hands around her tiny neck and squeeze the life out of her. I could see it: when I came to, blurred lights would be flashing around me, and I'd be standing in front of a camera, hearing muffled voices around me, and someone would be snapping my mug shot from several different angles.

But she wasn't worth it. In fact, none of this was. I had to be a woman, stand strong, and accept the fact that I had gotten myself into this mess, chasing ass and falling for a pretty face. And what's worse – falling for someone who was clearly detached and lacked concern for anyone besides herself and Katrina. My bad.

-Fifteen-

I spent the rest of the night at Gillian's in deep reflection, saddened that I'd allowed my life to get to that point. How dare I take out my anger on Angela when it was my fault alone for being in this situation? I could only hope that somehow God's mercy would be kind to me and that Angela or Katrina would not do something crazy concerning the contract and book deal. Given the fact that they both were unscrupulous bottom-feeders who took pleasure in eating people up and spitting them out gave me a lot to be worried about.

I felt cold and stale, and a stench of darkness that hovered over me sent shivers through my body. I scratched my skin and hair and held back tears that hung just inside my eyelids. I knew my status, whether Angela said so or not. She wasn't woman enough to be truthful to me, or maybe she and Katrina were more interested in making a quick buck, and I was just some casualty of their ongoing war.

My lips shook, and all the hair on my body stood straight up. Minutes turned into hours, and by noon the next day Gill came into her spare room and found me still sitting in the same spot - up against the wall, underneath the windowsill. I was an HIV-positive Black lesbian - one would think that statement to be an oxymoron that couldn't exist, but I beg to differ because anyone who thinks that our lifestyle is *privileged* needs to have his or her head examined. A risky lifestyle is a risky lifestyle, and if you sleep with dogs or bitches you are bound to get fleas: STD'S, HIV, and ultimately AIDS.

Dragging myself through the tight walls of Gillian's home, I followed her to the bathroom, where she had set out toiletries, a towel, and something for me to change into. I showered, dressed, and slipped out while she went to her room. Walking towards downtown Dallas, I barely looked up, and I continued on until my feet ached and I had no clue where I was. I thought about Waxahachie but dismissed the idea---wasn't in the mood to write or be soothed by the sounds of Rachelle Ferrell's astounding voice and gentle keystrokes that lately seemed to take me far away with no worries. It would only remind me of Angela and the first time I touched her with my mouth with no thought to protect myself or my heart.

I was in the middle of a Mexican neighborhood filled with colorful store signs and families running about, tending to their needs. I exhaled, reached for my cell, and called a cab service. I then stood there and took

in the beautiful scene of Hispanic culture that seemed to
be in a world of its own. The sounds of their accents as
mothers scolded their children, talked with friends, or
carried on phone conversations on their cell phones was
a stark contrast to how the world wanted to view this
group. With the immigration problems and an impending
election, I had to side with the Hispanics. They believed
in working for everything they wanted, and they were
here because they wanted to achieve the American Dream
- and who could blame them?

The yellow taxicab arrived, picked me up from the
corner of 10th Street, and proceeded to take me on a
thirty-dollar tab back to *Depression Ville*. When I arrived
home, I searched for my spare key underneath the
landscape fixture and let myself in.

I was so exhausted and worn down, Max and Moira
almost knocked me over. Had I known my encounter
with Angela would lead me back here, I would have
bypassed the puss, kept seeing my shrink, and called it a
day. Hell, I'd probably still have my job, be on good terms
with my folks, and not have some dreaded fate hanging
over my head.

Instead of beginning - like I suspected - my life
ended when I met Angela. I passed my blinking

answering machine and went into the bathroom, kicking off my shoes and getting stark naked, with Max and Moira in tow. I felt like a mad woman as I searched my cabinets and drawers for scissors, and when I found the cute split ends scissors, I commenced to cut my dreads until I was staring in the mirror at a lighter version of Buckwheat. Realizing that that wasn't enough to capture my fool-like behavior. I went "Brittany Spears," taking my old clippers and shaving my head completely. After awhile, I stopped looking. I then, turned on the water, took a quick shower, washed my ass, and went to bed.

I slept for what felt like an eternity, and if my dreams were any indication of what was to come, things were going to get bad real bad. *Sit up,* I told myself, then opened my eyes and looked into the bureau mirror at my light Caesar. I surveyed my shoulders, which seemed to slump a little, then looked at my breast. They seemed un-perky - if that's a word - and sad. Who was I fooling? I wanted to crawl into a ball and wither away; nonetheless, I peeled myself out of bed and went to the kitchen for some coffee.

Max and Moira were sleeping in their room, and I took in the stillness of my home.

"You're up," a soft voice said from behind me.

I turned, attempting to cover myself, only to see Gill standing there with her arms folded.

"Hey," I said, scratching my head and trying to figure out how she got in, as well as how long had she been there.

"I like the *do*...it fits you."

I grazed my hand over my shaven head, letting my bare body reflect in her eyes. She looked down and adjusted her arms.

"How'd you get in?"

"Oh, yeah, that...ahhh, you dropped your keys the other night, you know, when all of that stuff was going on. I grabbed them for you. I've been calling you, but you didn't answer; so, I figured I would just drop them off. No answer, though, and your dogs were barking like crazy - I mean *furiously*. I figured if you weren't here they were probably hungry and needed water, so the least I could do was feed them and let them out."

"That was brave."

"Yeah. I guess they remembered me or were glad for some food because they warmed right up to me."

"So much for having guard dogs...traitors." I said looking in their direction.

"Yeah, tell me about it."

"I can't believe I slept through all of that. Amazing."

"You did. I even covered you up."

"Really?"

"Un huh. Cleaned your bathroom up, too. By the way, I put your locks in a bag underneath your sink; didn't know if you wanted to keep them or throw them out."

I shook my head. As far as I was concerned, she could have burned them.

"You want some coffee?"

"Sure."

I turned my naked body around and fixed us some coffee while Gill tended to the dogs outside in the backyard.

"How do you like your coffee, Gill? " I called out to her.

"Plenty of cream and sugar."

"Brown sugar OK?"

"Perfect."

"Are you OK?" She asked, walking back into the kitchen as I poured the sugar in our coffee and added some crème. I walked over to the table and we sat and sipped in momentary silence.

"I'm fine. Superficial right?"

"What's that?" she asked.

"Thinking that I had found someone that I could love because she was pretty, had a nice body and was good in bed."

Gill shook her head in agreement and sipped again on her coffee. My kitchen seemed so spacious and emptiness filled the air. One thing was for certain, Angela was a huge mistake and soon enough, I had to face the consequences of my choices and being so damn superficial.

"Well if it helps, I never pegged you for superficial. In fact, I'd say you were the complete opposite. You just didn't get it right this time. Don't beat yourself up about it."

"Yeah, well I'm done I need to focus on my writing right now. I don't have time for all of the craziness and rules in this lifestyle. I mean when did it get so crazy that women have no regard for one another?"

"Not all women, like I said, you just didn't get it right this time."

"I never get it right. It's always something. You know it's been a long time since I allowed my self to get involved. I had a bad bout with major depression and just became a recluse. I was fighting so hard to beat it so I forced myself out for the first time in like two years and I met Angela.

She made me feel like writing again, and for the first time in soooo long, I had feelings below my waist. I felt alive again."

"Don't. Don't do this. Everything happens for a reason. And look, you're writing. Turn this around and make it work in your favor."

Gill had no clue. And I wasn't ready to tell her what the real issue was.

Part IV:

173

. . . all hell breaks loose . . .

-Sixteen-

Gill stayed for a few days and helped me put one foot in front of the other. She made sure the necessity was done like helping me go thru my mail. Checking my bank accounts to be sure bills were paid and that my mind was indeed wrapped tight. We had tons of coffee and tea, and she made me write for at least two hours each day. Fueled by anger alone, I finished the changes on the manuscript then let her do the remaining editing.

I met her handsome son, Josh, and I wasn't certain if he had a father or not; he looked more like her twin. Of course that being naturally impossible I thought about Gill's comment about having good genes. I smiled. He was a musician who played the sax, piano, and drums at his high school. He was talented and a true gentleman.

I had a court date in twenty days, and Gill helped me prepare for it. Katrina wanted to press charges against me for trespassing, and I wanted to dissolve my contract with them. I had never hit a woman before, and I was sure that I wasn't one of those emotionally or physically abusive lesbians who hit their women - but this time I wanted to beat both their asses.

I knew that I needed to see my therapist, but I

wasn't ready to disclose the whole story. Instead I decided to spend the weekend with Gill and Josh at my place.

Friday night we played monopoly for hours laughing and kidding around about Josh taking aloof our money then giving personal loans so the game wouldn't end. When the game finally ended and he did in fact win, we laughed some more. It was fun.

Josh had brought his Casio with his stand and bench and played soothing jazz music while Gill and I sat there in awe of his musical genius. He played like a he was a professional! He was truly gifted. He played one of my favorites the Classic *I can explain* followed by another Ferrell Classic *Nothing has ever felt like this before.*

It was obvious Gill knew how to appreciate good music and she had exposed her son to some of the greats. Even more surprising was Gills ex husband was a musician too and they had traveled a great deal. After a few more songs Gill and Josh told me about their time in Switzerland for the huge Jazz festival and how much fun they had there. We agreed that one day the three of us would go so I could take it all in. The way they talked about it had me on the edge of my seat in anticipation to be a part of something that sounded so beautiful.

From Quincy Jones, George Duke, Lauryn Hill to bands from all across the world people would for 16 days, go to venue after venue listening to good music. We lit the fireplace and drank hot cocoa and talked some more about going to the Montreux Jazz festival in Switzerland then one by one fell asleep. Gill and I each at the end of the sofa and Josh on the Chaise.

Saturday morning we fixed wheat waffles and had coffee and milk then sat out side in lounge clothes and heavy jackets while the dog played and the outside fireplace crackled as the fresh wood burned. By noon we had all slipped into our private worlds and took naps respectively.

I woke up to the sounds of Josh on his Alto saxophone toying around with some music he and his dad were working on. It was so angelic and graceful. I washed my face and went to join him and listen while Gill smiled at me from the kitchen as she prepared us some baked fish and fresh vegetables.

His musical piece was fascinating. I closed my eyes sat back on the couch and just listened until he stopped and Gill stood over me smiling.

"Hey Mom, Remember this one?" Josh said the broke into the Herman Kelly classic holding the initial note then blowing on that Saxophone like he was a full-grown man. Gill lifted her arms and hands and twisting her body like the holy spirit hit her. Yet she danced with perfect poise, swaying her hips to his horns and her memory and shook her head sweetly. Her body was slender and toned from countless hours running and moving with the beat of life. She was radiant a picture perfect cut out of healthy living. Peace and serenity.

I smiled from ear to ear he was great and she was---breathtaking. I thought about the other instruments that made that song so powerful, the drums, bass guitar and those things you shake that sounds like huge salt shakers. Gill's rhythm and Josh's gift was special. This day would live in my heart and mind forever.

"It's dinner time---this concert is over." Gill said as his rendition came to and end and she was all smiles. Proud. She said it so calmly---she wasn't even out of breath after all that dancing and moving her head from side to side. Had that been me, I'd been asking for oxygen after fifteen seconds into the song.

I smiled back. It was like a concert I had to admit. This was one of those surreal moments that only happen once in a while. I continued to smile and we all went to the kitchen and sat giving thanks for another day and a well prepared meal.

Somewhere in the middle of my meal I began to twinge with anger as thoughts of Katrina and Angela began to fill my head. The thoughts were pecking me like a woodpecker against wood. I couldn't shake them. The entire fiasco about court and the contract made me feel constrained and held back, standing still while I took the pecks. My mood had changed and Gill noticed it.

"You know, you have to get out of this house. You have cabin fever. Why don't we go to the movies? Or the three of us can go looking at Christmas lights in Ovilla."

"Not going to happen. I'm tired."

"From what? Sleeping too much? Come on, Claude, you need to."

"You two go. I'm just going to stay in for a while and get my head together. You know, eventually I'll have to find a job." I said excusing myself from the table and going into my office and sitting on my couch in there. Gill followed and stood in the doorway.

"You won't need a job; this book is your ticket, Claude."

"Yeah, you think my agent will see to that?" I said in a sarcastic tone, rolling my eyes.

"This is just as huge for you as it is for them. Trust me."

"That's why they won't let me out of this contract - that damn Katrina wants blood," I said, almost gritting my teeth.

"Angela is about business and making money."

"I don't want to make money for them. I'd rather not."

"Remember, I'm part of that company too."

I rolled my eyes again. I had been meaning to tell Gillian that I wasn't comfortable with that either, considering Katrina's mess. I sat back on the couch wring my hands and looked up at the ceiling. I couldn't tell my mother why I hated my father, and Gill was clueless about everything. She was so damn optimistic it was starting to drive me crazy. I was more interested in that damn woodpecker in my head!

"I need to be alone, Gill. I just have too many things on my mind right now." I was beginning to think I had two personalities. First I wanted her and Josh there so I can avoid seeking help from my therapist and suddenly I felt like walls were closing in around me and needing to be alone. I was truly struggling.

"Are you sure?" she said, sitting beside me on the

sofa.

"Yes."

"Well since you don't want to go out, I'm going to drop Josh off with his Dad and meet a friend for some drinks. I'll call you tomorrow?" she said with a smile.

Gill stroked my hands and she and Josh left. Hearing the door shut and hearing her and Josh say goodbye was heartbreaking. I really didn't want them to leave. It would have been great going to see the Christmas lights in Ovilla. Looking at those big houses and being surrounded by friends. Instead she was going on a date and I was stuck on stupid sitting on my couch, wringing my hands and mad that I had a court date with Katrina and Angela.

-Seventeen-

The following week I stayed in and avoided Gill. She had called a few times to check on me and talk to me about some blind date she went on. It was fun she said and she and the woman hit it off. I told her that was nice and found any excuse to end our conversation. *Let me call you back Max has gotten out of the house, let me call you back my toilet is stopped up, let me call you back someone's at the door.*

My mother called on one of those days after I had lied to Gill and I was ready to lay on big lie so Gill could just leave me alone. But instead Mom told me that Uncle Peter died alone at a hospice in Kingston and my father was headed to Jamaica to finish up his affairs. No family members, old friends, people from his hometown, or former teammates were by his side, and there was no huge, traditional *Ni'nite* to commemorate his lifetime achievements. It was just him and his attending nurse, who saw him take his last breath early that Sunday morning. She told me that Aunt Carol had called to share the news, saying, *"Uncle Peter ded im gwaan no feneral."*

Part of me was angry with her, too. So what if Uncle Peter was gay? What about us being a family? More importantly, do they shun all outsiders? And, if so, what about my father's bastard children, running around Jamaica while his wife and daughter lived a complete lie in the states? How come that wasn't an issue?

I managed to muster up a headache big enough to force me to collapse into a deep sleep. In dream after dream, I saw my scrawny father talking off in the distance. He had a look on his face that made my skin crawl - even in my dreams. They say we don't dream in color, but I could have sworn I saw him dressed in red, his locks a bronze and dirty gray, and his teeth a dingy hue. If I walked ten paces, we would be face-to-face, but for some reason I couldn't move.

And apparently neither could he. He just stood there off in the distance with his mouth slightly open, showing those yellow teeth. No matter what I was dreaming about, he'd be right there, standing off in the distance.

Then I dreamt that I had made love to Angela, kissed Gillian, fought ferociously with Katrina, and still I saw my father - scrawny and sporting yellow teeth - standing there. The only way I shook him was when I was with Uncle Peter, walking through the park in the midst of fog as we laughed and held hands. He let go of my hands, and I wanted to grab his strong hand again, but he pulled away. Smiling, he walked on into the fog, and my heart sank. For the first time in all my life, I cried in my sleep, so much so that I awoke with tears still wet on my face. I used my shirt to wipe my eyes and face, then went into the kitchen to fix some coffee. Startled, I almost peed in my pants as I saw my mother sitting at my table with tears rolling down her soft pink cheeks.

"Your aunt called back; they can't find your father."

"What do you mean, they can't find him?"

"Sweetie, please; don't make this more difficult."

"Mom, please. He went to Jamaica to take care of Uncle Peter's business, and now Aunt Carol or no one else knows where he is? Does that sound right to you? Come on. This is bull-crap."

"Claude, you watch your mouth - and how do you think I feel? This is my husband we are talking about, not just your father. Do you know what I am feeling right now? Do you? You are being selfish, childish, and immature ..."

Mom's eyes were heavy with tears, which started to fall uncontrollably. It's a wonder how she was able to speak in damn near complete sentences; but, make no mistake, I had crossed the line and completely forgotten that her life would be turned upside down. Her face was weary, like she hadn't slept because thoughts about what happened to Dad kept racing through her mind. Words left me, and I was stuck looking deep into her eyes. I felt like crap, and she walked out just as quietly as she had come in.

-Eighteen-

Five days after my mother had sat at my kitchen table, neither of us had bothered to check on one another and I had no idea if she had even searched for my father. I don't know what her reasons were, but as far as I was concerned he was a liar, had a double life, and didn't give a crap about gay people - even his own daughter. For the past four nights, I had cried myself to sleep, thinking about how he had placed me in a box and expected me to never come out to my people in Jamaica, or how he shared a bond with his other children, which was clearly obvious when we last went home together.

On night number three, I promised myself that I would never live in someone's box and never *not* love someone for the sake of someone else. More importantly, I vowed never to live a life that was a lie. I was a natural lesbian, a Jamaican and Jewish lesbian with no hair - bald. My mother had nothing to do with it, nor did my father; it was simply who I was. Period. That's the end of my story.

I sat there with my dogs, missing Uncle Peter and cussing my father, when the doorbell rang and Max and Moira went ballistic. I hurried to get the door.

"DHL," the voice said, and I opened the door and slid my body out before the dogs could rip the deliveryman apart.

"Delivery for Claudette R. Moore."

"I'm Claude Moore."

"Perfect. I just need your signature here." He handed me the electronic signature device, and I complied. He jogged back to his van and retrieved a small envelope, then came back, handed it to me, and went on his merry way.

It was from Mandeville. *Strange*, I thought, then tossed it on the counter and began to dress so I could go to the Whole Foods for some fresh flowers, fruit, and Greek olives for a Mediterranean salad I planned to fix later. It was time to beat this stroll down pity lane!

My cell phone rang; it was my mother's ring tone: "I'll Always Love My Momma," by the O'Jays. I let out a deep sigh, hoping that I could be considerate of her love for my father and continue to hide my disgust for him, missing or not.

"Hello, Mother, how are you?"

"Claudette -" that wasn't a good sign - calling me by my full name - and she sounded like she was talking to one of her students.

"Yes?"

"They found his body…your father…I received the telegram today with official word that he…" she paused, and it felt like she was trying to hold back this time, "was found dead there."

The moment those words left her mouth my mind left me. I felt emotionless and the blood in my veins seemed to run cold. I wanted to slam down the phone and shut the world out. He left us with no answers.

I managed to hide my lack of emotion and asked, "Mom, how are you?"

"Claude, sweetheart, how are you, baby?"

"I'm well, considering. What about you? Are you holding up okay?"

"Well---" she paused. "I guess it was unexpected. I mean, I just don't know." I heard her voice get heavy again. I knew this was tearing her up, and there was nothing I could do. My father went back to Jamaica and got himself killed in a "freak" accident. No one would talk about it, so basically she was left with no answers, not knowing the truth about my father's secret life.

"Are you going to catch a flight? Head down there?"

"Flight? Humph…there isn't going to be a flight. Your relatives - precisely *Aunt Carol* - thinks it would be best if *I* or *WE* didn't show up for his funeral."

"What? Are you serious?"

I wanted so bad to spill the beans on my fraudulent family. My mother was his fool and now they had the nerve to bar her from his funeral. What a slap in the face, kick in the groin and every other disrespectful deed.

"Well, Claude, if you'd called sooner than now you'd know this."

"Don't start, Mom. You know I've been upset with him, and it's not like he bothered to call me either."

"And now look; he's gone, and the two of you have unresolved issues." She sad sadly.

"Not exactly I have my own issues, which I've been meaning to talk to you about."

"What issues - and let me remind you, your father has passed away, and neither of us can be a part of his burial, funeral, and whatever else they do in Jamaica. It's like we don't exist." She said loudly.

Got that right, I wanted so bad to tell her. My father was a liar, and, quite frankly, I could care less about him dying and only wanting his Jamaican family to be a part of his burial.

I guess that explains the DHL delivery. I was shutting down. "Look, Mom, I gotta go."

"Claude?"

"Yeah, Mom?"

"I don't know what I'm going to do without him."

I pressed the "end" button and placed the receiver down. I looked around the room before turning my table upside down, throwing the lamps across the room and throwing the receiver as hard as I could. I didn't stop there, I made my way to the kitchen throwing dishes, glasses and pictures of my family before sliding down the pantry door and sobbing like I was five and just told I couldn't get the big wheel that I wanted for my birthday.

-Nineteen-

So what does one say when a no-good father has turned up dead and his kin doesn't want you or his wife around? I had to consider that all of the folks back in Mandeville - and wherever else our family was scattered - knew about my father's other life. But, what I didn't understand was why someone would choose to be so deceitful to my mother, who I'm sure wouldn't harm a soul.

She had a presence about her that made me better; it's like she saw something good in every human being and shined her "light" so to speak, on them so that they could be more, have more, and ultimately do more. And, as much as I would rather not admit this, I knew that if she had met Angela she would have adored her and brought her better side out. She might have even been able to turn Katrina's thwarted soul around, too.

I could only sigh because just the thought of Katrina and Angela suddenly made my chest tight and my upper lip twitch. I zoned in on the two of them sitting back somewhere, laughing at me while I contemplated going to the Health Department. They probably took out a life insurance policy on me and were waiting for me to kick the bucket. Better yet, they probably had Gill around to finish off the plan - *meanwhile*, back on the ranch, I'm thinking she's on my side.

I bet those two skanks were going to run off with all of the proceeds from my books and probably wipe my name off my latest manuscript, leaving me to die somewhere in London or Harlem on skid row. Those bitches! I mouthed through clenched teeth and bawled up fists.

My heart felt like it was going to jump through my chest, and I felt sweat on my temples beginning to slide down my face. I jumped from the sofa and made my way to the computer to check the signs and symptoms of being HIV-positive.

There were tons and tons of hits, everything from statistics, the highest group of affected individuals, and problems in the gay and lesbian communities, with lesbians being targeted because of the increase of bisexuality - or at least that was what one site said. I didn't really agree with that; I guess I was more concerned with people who were promiscuous and careless overall, which didn't necessarily mean bisexual people.

I thumbed through a dozen more sites, trying to

ease my racing mind, when I stumbled upon:

- *rapid weight loss*

- *dry cough and shortness of breath*

- *chronic fatigue*

- *swollen lymph nodes in the armpits or neck*

- *spots on the tongue, mouth, the nose, or on the eyelids*

- *pneumonia*

- *memory loss*

- *lasting depression and other neurological disorders*

The following medical conditions can also be in connection with an HIV infection:

- *fever (longer than one month)*

- *night sweats (longer than one month)*

- *diarrhea (longer than one month)*

I cut off the computer in such a fury you'd thought I was surfing the net on some forbidden site because I knew that at least three or four of the things on the list had consumed me since Angela had told me about Katrina, then lied and said that she herself wasn't positive. I was dropping weight like I had taken on the habit of mixing meth and crack and indulging in the deadly mixture three to five times a day!

My clothes fit me like a potato sack, and the bags that were beginning to show up under my eyes made me want to crawl up somewhere and just die. I moved slowly to my bedroom like the character from the Green Mile *Dead man walking---Dead man walking* ---and let the sweat drip from my body, as I got into bed and I just laid in it and drifted off to sleep. Sleep was my only remedy if only I didn't dream such vivid dreams.

-Twenty-

Gill came by a couple days later we cleaned up the mess I made then dragged me out of the house. I needed it. I was falling a part and the condition of my home and office was proof.

It was the weekend of my birthday. She remembered and said I needed to get out to celebrate and get used to my baldhead (which now went way beyond a light Caesar) and all of the stares. In fact, she was determined to get me to deal with all of the looks and stares, taking me to an all-boy's party at J. Pepes, which was sponsored by a group of affluent, well-to-do Black folk who knew how to throw a party. She wanted to celebrate the fact the Katrina and Angela had dropped all of the charges, and, deep down inside, I wanted to, too.

When we got there, it was wall-to-wall men throughout the place, all types of beautiful Black men who were dressed to impress and smelling like a million bucks. There wasn't a single ugly guy there, and all of them had muscles that bulged through different hues of turtlenecks, ribbed shirts, sweaters, tweed blazers, and fine button down oxfords.

I had to admit, the atmosphere was welcoming and cheerful; a stark contrast to how I had been feeling. I smiled instantly as men complimented my new hairstyle, as well as the style of attire that I'd chosen for the evening: a navy suit with a striped Oxford, a Cardigan vest that offset the shirt, and a pair of fresh, clean Adidas that pulled it all together.

I thought about Uncle Peter as I danced with the MC and a couple other confident guys, wondering how many gay nightspots he had partied at, given his status as a semi-pro athlete. I also wondered if Jamaica even had such places for him to party. Uncle Peter would have fit in just fine here; his chiseled body, deep dimples, and beautiful mocha skin made him look like an Adonis, and in his bright whites he was always dressed to impress. Yep, he'd fit right in.

"Dance with me," Gill leaned in and said to me from behind. She almost pushed me over, and I knew she had partaken of some of the devil's wine. Her words simmered on the nape of my neck and lingered there. Her soft hand grazed my head, and I turned to face her dreamy doe eyes. She kept her hand around my neck, pulling me close to her, and I inhaled hints of cognac and patchouli. Her lips seemed to glisten as she slowly licked them, looking deep into my eyes. Our bodies touched, and it was almost electric; there was warm energy that radiated from her. Cheek-to-cheek, and with her breast against mine, we settled into one another with a slow, sensual grind. She then grabbed one of my hands and led me to the small of her back. The sounds of old school music and bodies gyrating were hypnotic, and for a moment I forgot all about Angela and my woes.

Yet, I suddenly pushed away from Gill, saying, "I gotta get home - just remembered I have some stuff to work on for my mother." That was a lie.

"What did you say?" she said over the music, which was so loud that, if I hadn't been watching her lips so hard, I couldn't tell what she had said.

I motioned to the door and walked off the dance floor. I then found the exit in a hurry, trying to make my escape, but two buff dudes stopped me in my tracks and pointed behind me; I had to face her.

"Where are you going? It's just a little after twelve." Her voice wasn't strained; it was filled with concern, and maybe a little hurt.

"I just remembered I have to take care of something for my mother."

Her beautiful deep eyes were mesmerizing,

complimenting her tan skin. She was shiny and glowed in her navy fitted dress and lapis jewelry, which rested on her cleavage. She was simply beautiful.

"I'll call you tomorrow. We can do lunch or something?"

"Okay," she softly said, and I dared not hug or touch her again. I turned away quickly and almost sprinted to my car. Once inside, I sighed deeply, grateful that we had driven separate cars. I should have known that was coming when we both met up at the club looking like a couple in our matching navy blue.

I drove home with visions of Gill in my head; the dreadlocks afro and her natural beauty, which seemed so pure and strong-willed. She was a wise, intelligent, beautiful black woman. I couldn't help wondering why I couldn't have met someone like her instead of Angela. Why was I always choosing the wrong woman and clearly letting the good ones slip through my hands like sand?

Then there were the thoughts of my damn father, who had the nerve to run back to Jamaica and get himself killed, leaving both me and Mom to wonder about what kind of lie we had been living all this time. I reached for my cell phone and called her.

"Hey, Mom. You sleep?"

"No; reading…and you aren't asleep because…?"

"Went out with Gill for a little bit. I didn't feel like staying. You have some coffee on?"

"I do. Are you coming by?"

"Yes. I'll be there in a second."

"Okay, dear."

My mother was iron-willed; she didn't let the entire fiasco with my dad ruin her. In fact, she had displayed enormous strength since he died and his relatives gave us the cold shoulder. She had her tenured career at the university, solid friendships, and a crap load of money saved. More importantly, she was a Jewish woman with strong convictions and very close to her family. I wish I could be half the woman she was.

I drove to the back of the house and let myself in. A two-seat, flashy red Benz had replaced my dad's old truck, alongside my mother's modest Volvo.

Well, she's spending money, I thought, but I wasn't sure if that was good or not.

"Mom," I called to her from the back door. The smell of my father still lingered through the house; it was a mixture of old spice and cigar that met me at the back door. I couldn't help but think of all the lies he told and his double life - not to mention the fact that he did nothing to help Uncle Peter, yet he supposedly supported me and my lifestyle. *LIAR!*

"We're in the kitchen."

Who's in the kitchen? Surely, she wasn't shacking' up already? I wasn't in the mood for that; it had only been three weeks since Dad's death. I wanted to turn right back around, but I didn't. I walked into the kitchen, and Mom was in her robe with her glasses on, fixing a fresh pot of coffee.

"Who's '*WE?*'" I asked.

"Hi, sweetheart. Julia's gone to put her robe on."

"Who the hell is Julia?"

"Watch your tone, young lady, and grab the crème from the refrigerator."

I did as my mother asked, rolling my eyes in my head and trying to remember who the heck was Julia? That name did not ring a bell - but... *J* did. I turned around with the crème in my hand, and my mouth and jaw slightly dropped. I guess the conversation about my head being shaved was going to have to wait.

"Hello, Claude," she said, "it's finally nice to meet you." She seemed familiar, like she had been a part of my family all along. It seemed as though she levitated into the kitchen, and my feet fell like lead, my mouth dried up, and the frog that usually became stuck in everyone else's throat suddenly got stuck in mine!

"Claude, this is Julia…" My mother wanted to say more, but she could tell by the look on my face that I probably wasn't ready to hear that my mother's friend - or 'rich gentleman caller', as she so pointedly put it - was indeed a woman and that the only reason she was with my father was that at the time she couldn't be with Julia. Was this karma? Or genetic? No wonder I had found lying so damn easy at times.

"Nice to meet you, Julia," I said, trying not to stutter or appreciate her stunning beauty. *Such a dedicated woman to wait on my mother all these years.* I surveyed her hands and saw no wedding ring; just the same ring my mother wore on her right ring finger.

Julia took over the coffee fixing and made three cups, then we sat and drank in silence - until Mom asked about Angela.

"So, have you spoken to her?"

"No, she and I are done. She's back with her partner; I guess this time for good."

"What about the book?"

"Yeah," Julia chimed in, "what are you going to do about the contract?"

"I don't know. I signed with them and turned over a manuscript almost two months ago. I haven't heard anything or heard from her."

"And the editor - this Gill chick. Does she know anything?"

"She says I need not worry. One thing Angela and Katrina are into is making money. And I don't even care; if they screw me - and it is quite possible they will - I'll just take some time off and start over. Maybe Cindy can give me another connection or contact."

"Well, I hope it works out for you."

"Me, too, and at least they dropped the charges." I said, taking my last sip of coffee then realizing I hadn't told my mother everything.

"Charges?"

I waved my hand and then said, "I will tell you later---long story."

My mother sighed then stood and grabbed our cups. I could only hope that my excuse to talk about it later would suffice. It did.

"Sweetie, are you going to stay? Julia and I have an early morning, so we must retire. Breakfast tomorrow? Julia makes awesome flapjacks."

I smiled. My mom was getting laid by a woman and rushing me out the door.

"No, I just came to check on you. Glad everything is okay."

I stood and planted a soft kiss on her cheek.

"Goodnight, Julia." I said, then kissed her as well.

"Goodnight, sweetheart," Mom said, then Julia reached out her hand and took mine and said, "*The Ladder.* Your ladder isn't broken; true love does exist."

I smiled and left the two of them there.

My ladder was broken, destroyed, and scattered in a million pieces across some desert. Even my mother was experiencing true love with a woman, and I was wilting away - probably at death's door.

-Twenty-One-

I sat at home, wondering about Gill and the fact that we had almost kissed. Thoughts of my mother and Julia, my father, life without Angela, and the unknown - as far as my status - were heavy on my mind. Two months after having seen Gill, Mom, and Julia, I hastened myself to get back out and go back to where Gill and I had gone - *The Bar.*

Thoughts of her were the only ones that seemed to soothe me: the closeness I felt when her body grazed mine and I inhaled her, in a sense inhaling her essence. I didn't want to jump her bones, but her closeness left me yearning for more - in a different kind of way.

I pulled myself from bed, got dressed, and headed to where it all took place - *The Bar.* While driving, I listened to a Sound-Scape CD and thought more of Gill, and tucked away in my thoughts was the hope that Gill was nothing like Angela or that God-forsaken Katrina. That alone almost made me want to turn back around - but I didn't.

The same old bar that sat right off I35 had a parking lot full of cars. As I turned my car off, I could hear the sounds of music. Hesitantly, I went in. It was a masquerade ball with a bevy of women on hand; I knew this from seeing tresses hang from behind their masks and enough cleavage to make me want to put on some damn shades. Finding Gill was going to be tough; more so, who's to say she was at this particular event?

I ignored the stares and nods and made my way through the *fire*; it was hot and moist, and hints of perfumed bodies filled the air. Through blinking masquerades and sultry lips, I searched for Gill, hoping that her essence and aura would stand out. A chilly day in February and just shy of Valentine's, the inside of the bar was no comparison to what the weather was like outside.

It almost felt like an out-of-body experience as I floated through the crowd; I saw myself looking through masks, licking my lips, and scrutinizing each figure, trying to identify Gill and her eyes through the mask. The nape of my neck felt moist - like penetrating eyes had pierced right through me - and I stopped in my tracks, turned around, and rubbed my hand across my moist baldhead.

The mask woman who I thought was following me just stood there with her eyes gazing over me, simmering with seduction. Moving closer to her, I reached for her mask, then she grabbed my hand, kissed the center of it, and held it against her cheek. I proceeded to unmask her – and saw that it was Gill. She had seen me when I walked in and watched as I scanned the bar in search of her.

Our lips met, pressing against one another - and it was like I knew her, knew something so intimate about her. I liked it. Together we explored one another's tongue and softly kissed; innocently, yet passionately. We kissed for sometime like it was New Years Eve, or our wedding day and standing still as the sunset and we were exchanging vows.

Then her purse touched my side, vibrating and interrupting our moment.

"One sec," she said, lifting her finger up, "expecting a text from my son."

I smiled and let out a relaxing sigh. I looked around the bar, which now seemed more relaxed, and watched moving heads, whispering bodies, and moving hands. My out-of-body experience came back, and Gill pulled on my arm and hand and led me out of the bar. Our pace was quickening, and I thought surely this place was on its way down. Once we were out the door, the cold air hit me like a freight train, and Gill seemed flustered and weak, making gasping noises like she wanted to puke. I reached to hold her, and she pushed me away, like she needed to break free.

"Gill, what's the matter?"

"No, no - NOOOOOOO!" Gill yelled, and I froze with fear. Did she know? Did she really think she could catch the virus from a kiss?

"She, she's..." she said, "she's been hurt. She did this to her. I told her to leave her alone."

I reached for her, making her look at me and repeat what she had just said.

"She's at the burn unit at Parkland. Katrina doused her with gasoline and set her on fire . . ." Gill said more, but I was like a deck of playing cards that someone had tapped, helplessly falling to the ground - and Gill fell, too.

Part V:

. . . and now she's gone.

212

-Twenty-Two-

I guess I was stronger than I thought. Someone put me to bed at Gill's, and when I woke up the brightness of her room calmed me. I crawled up in a ball and waited for Gill. I let tears fall from my eyelids while those haunting words played back in my head, each time finding strength in a world so cold and evil, one so filled with hate that even in our small community one of us would do this to one of our own. Surely, it was not love that held those two together, but hate, jealousy, and all the things I detest.

Gill's door opened slightly, and I peeked up to see her son, who shut the door as soon as he opened it. I wiped my face and went to the other room to talk to him.

"Hey, Josh." I said wiping my face

"Good afternoon," he said politely. He was the fine young man that his parents raised well today and not Josh the musician that belted out tunes and played his keyboard like it was with him when he was born.

"Where's Gill?"

"She's with Dad at the hospital."

"Is she okay?"

"He left his number so you could call him. Call

him," he ordered and half-smiled as I took the number from his hand.

I grabbed my cell phone from the room and dialed the number. He answered on the first ring.

"Claude," he said in his strong voice.

"Sir?" I replied, unsure of what to say.

He let out a deep sigh and began to tell me things I did not want to hear. He said that Gill was at the hospital, something about shock and Angela - Angela's loud screams and murmurs when she was taken away...Katrina dead...it was too much to handle. The doctors said her mind couldn't take it, and she literally checked out.

Then I began to remember vividly our rushing to the hospital after someone whisked us away from the club and we sped quietly to Parkland. I stared into space while Gill did the same. The driver dropped us off at the emergency entrance and we double-timed inside. Then my feet felt like I was walking on Rhino Glue as I saw the back of Gills body jerk as sounds of gun fire went off rapidly. It was like we were in the middle of the streets of a civil war.

My feet stopped moving and my knees gave out as I watched Katrina's head explode like a watermelon thrown against a concrete sidewalk. Splat! Her body shrinking as she melted into the hospital floor in a pool of blood.

Katrina - in her desperate need to be some martyr or superhero - ended it all in front of Gill and I, and the hospital staff; coward. She still wasn't woman enough to accept losing, even in the end.

The armed security officers had been summoned to the area when Katrina came in wielding a 9mm pistol and demanding to see Angela only seconds before we arrived. She was shot twice in the knees before she turned the pistol on her self. We witnessed it all.

Katrina's picture would be in the morning newspaper alongside Angela with the byline: *Jilted Lover, douses partner with gasoline then kills herself at the same hospital.*

I listened as Josh's dad's voice seemed to trail off, and when he asked me to stay with their son until Gill came home my mind and thoughts became clear again.

"Sure. Anything you guys need," Hanging up the phone, I smiled at their son and motioned to him that I'd be right back. I went into Gill's room, shut the door, pressed my back against it, and slid down. Holding my knees tightly while I cried at the mess we were ALL suddenly in. This entire fiasco was a result of Angela not leaving a relationship that was detrimental to her and Katrina not being woman enough to accept when someone no longer loves you.

I wished for sleep, my mother's wisdom, strength, and my father's presence; I sure was going to need it.

-Twenty-Three-

One year later. . .

Since Katrina's suicide and the attempted murder of Angela, Gill and I had remained close. She beat her setback of being shocked by helping me. I stayed with her some days and nights, and she would stay with me on weekends when her son was at his dad's. People say there is strength in numbers; I guess, to some extent. I was attempting to repair my broken ladder...attempting.

Yet I was still harboring a secret, still afraid to drag myself down to the Health Department and check my status, too afraid to cry on my mother's shoulder and tell her of my possible fate. I was a strong coward - if there could even be one - and the attempts of me repairing my broken ladder seemed to be in vain.

The only good thing was that Gill and I spent countless hours working on more of my manuscripts, revising and collaborating. I loved that she was such a worker bee and that she inspired me to write, to write with passion and with all of my might. It was like she was my guardian angel and never left my side. I had someone to come home to, talk to, be sad with, and someone to watch over me so that I could get a peaceful night's sleep with no interruptions from nightmares of being HIV-positive.

Or of seeing a charcoaled Angela standing there, looking at me, wanting to say something – but she never would. And I had someone I could watch over too. We took turns caring for each other but never crossing the line of intimacy ever again.

Meanwhile, my mother and Julia had moved in together, which I never thought was possible...never.

She'd check in every now and again while she was enjoying her sabbatical, doing public speaking and promoting women's rights, gay and lesbian rights, particularly the right to marriage.

My mother, the crusader, and her lover by her side made me nervous. She had forgotten all about my father...his death...that, I couldn't understand either.

Summer had come and gone again, and the anniversary of Angela's fate was creeping up on me. I felt it inside, which scared me, too. I wasn't sure if I ever loved her or not, if I hated her for dragging me on an escapade that ultimately led to death, or if I simply despised her for playing with my heart, then throwing it all away when it was convenient for her. Like it was some tryst I think I hated her, hated what she had carelessly done.

"Claude," Gill's soft voice called to me as I lay on the sofa in my office. She had pleasantly snapped me out of my thoughts. As usual, she was so thoughtful and considerate.

"Yeah?" I said, turning to look at her.

"Telephone," she said with a smile, shaking the cordless receiver in her hand. I sighed, knowing it was my mother with some news about her movement and what she and her lover had been up to and yadda yadda yadda as far as the townspeople, politicians etc., etc. I almost wanted to motion to Gill that I was asleep or not in. I pulled myself from the sofa and whispered, "Who is it?" as I walked towards her.

She shrugged with a smile; that meant it was Mom - and I wasn't in the mood. I quickly thought of an excuse to end the call as I grabbed the receiver.

"Hello?" I said firmly, trying to sound hurried or busy.

"Claudette."

My heart pounded in my chest, and my knees were weak.

"Good night," he said, as if he were straining to talk to me. "It's you fader, Claudette."

"My who?" I shot back, trying to hear his voice again. I knew it sounded like him. My heart felt like it was him, but I had to hear him say it again.

"It's you fader - me need to talk to you. Meyah in Jamaica in prison. Me no worry you and your mother. Ifa me call you it make me sad. Me yah coming home bebee. My wan you to pick me up from deh airport on Saturday."

Remaining silent, I shifted my eyes to Gill. She seemed hopeful, with her doe eyes full of support and a smile on her face that said, *It's okay.*

"Dad," I managed to get out, holding back the cry in my voice, "they said you died."

"No meyah had to pay a debt. Mixed up in political mess. Me no opposition or threat to my people."

I had so many questions, and my mind began to jump and flicker. My mother being a lesbian, his other children, and the fact that my aunts had lied to me and forbade us to come to check on him and give him a proper burial.

"It's a secret, Claudette. Mi can't tell or deh be in trouble. Mi so sorry."

"Where are you now, Dad?"

"Mi still in prison. Get out day after tomorrow. You pick mi up eh?"

I couldn't believe it - my father was alive, and I was standing there in the middle of my office, talking to him. My heart began to beat rapidly, and a light dizziness snuck up on me like a viper. I couldn't fight it anymore, I collapsed.

Shaking me and slapping me all in the same motion, Gill finally got me to wake up.

"I think my father is alive," I muttered. It was like something was caught in my throat and my pale office walls were closing in on me.

"Was that him? He had a very strong accent. I had to ask him twice who was he calling for."

"He wants me to pick him up from the airport..." I paused, "this can't be right---he also mentioned some woman named Patrina would be there as well." I shook my head. My father had the nerve to resurface from the dead and tell me some crap about meeting some woman Patrina at the airport!

"Who's that?" Gill asked, snapping me out of my daze.

"Who the hell knows?" The phone rang again and interrupted my thoughts.

"Hello?" I said with a hint of anger in my voice, hoping that it was my father and that I could let him know exactly how I felt about his request – as well as the fact that he'd just resurfaced from the dead.

"Claude, sweetheart, it's Mom."

"Oh, hey, Mom. How are you?"

She sighed, and I had to wonder if she'd just received the same call that I had.

"Your father..." her voiced sounded heavy and filled with uncertainty. She had some secrets of her own that she had to face with my father. Part of me understood her pain, part of me did not. She had lied about who she was, too. All of these lies and all of the hurt that came with them; it just didn't seem worth it anymore.

"You okay, Mom?" I asked, trying to conceal my ambiguity.

"Sweetheart, he's alive..." her voice went low, as if she were going hoarse. "He's alive," she said again, and I could hear the cry in her voice and see the tears running down her slightly aging skin.

"I know. I just received a call from him, too. Mom, I don't know what's going on. He wants me to pick him up at the airport - the day after tomorrow. Sunday."

"I'm going with you."

"Are you sure? Me and Gill can take care of this."

"I'm sure."

"Mom, he said some woman is supposed to meet us there, too." I was telling everything. I almost couldn't wait to rub in my father's face, the fact that my mother was playing for my team - liar or not, I was such a hypocrite; I guess I earned that right honestly.

"I know. She's some lawyer from Jamaica. He said something about his cellmate he's trying to help. That's just like your father, thinking about others when things are so crazy for him. I can't believe they held him in that prison all this time, allowing no contact with us."

I wanted to interject because she clearly did not know my father like she thought she did. He had another family, and, in the eyes of the United States of America, if he were married to that wench in Jamaica, he was breaking the law.

"We need to talk, Mom. How about we meet for breakfast before we pick him up? There's something I need to tell you."

"Okay, sweetheart. Everything okay?"

"Yeah," I lied---again. "I just want to talk about some things that have been eating at me, is all."

"Oh, okay. Surely. Are you coming to my place? I'm leaving Canada in the morning; should be home late tomorrow evening."

"Okay. I'll be home - I mean, by yawl's place at about eight in the morning."

"That's fine, sweetheart. I will see you then."

"OK, Mom. I love you. Bye."

"I love you, too. Bye, sweetheart."

I sighed heavily and hung up the phone. It was time that I came clean and told my mother about the burden I was carrying and the truth about my father and his family in Jamaica.

"She seems to be taking this fairly well," Gill said, and again I had to snap out of my zone. I was so comfortable having her around that I had forgotten so many times that she was there. She was like a permanent fixture in my life that I was used to, and no matter what she was always going to be there.

"Yeah, surprisingly. I wonder how she plans on telling him about her lover." I had to shake my head again. I was doing that a lot lately. I was just at such a loss for words. I wonder if being at a loss for words was a symptom of HIV. Why was I so afraid to even look into this? Coward. Plain and simple.

After Angela, I had transformed into a coward. She had broken me, broken me down into a zillion pieces, and I was walking around with my head turned around 180 degrees, aloof about everything. Had it not been for Gill, I'd need a straightjacket!

The phone rang again. "Can you grab that please, Gill? I can't do another family moment with my folks right now."

"Are you sure?"

"Yeah. Tell them I'm in the shower or taking a crap. Well, don't say 'anything,' just tell them I'll call them back."

"Hello?" Gill sung in a soft voice. She was so pleasant and warm. I smiled, watching her professionalism and care radiate throughout the room, her eyes darting quickly, and the sudden change in her tone.

"Well, hello. How are you?"
I looked puzzled, and she motioned for me to come towards her.

"I'm better. No complaints. I'm glad to hear you are okay." Her voice became filled with empathy and compassion, and I thought, *Wow, my Mom is going to love this girl. She's so sweet.*

"Yes, she's here." She motioned for me again to come closer to the phone; I rolled my eyes in my head.

"No," I mouthed to her and shook my head and waved my hand, but Gill looked at me pensively and handed me the phone.

"Hello?" I said with an attitude. I didn't know if I were more upset with Gill or the person on the phone.

"Claude," came from the familiar voice.

I pushed my ear to the phone, listened in, and said, "Angela?"

"Yes."

There was a pause that seemed to last for an eternity.

"How are you?"

"I'm okay.----- How are you?" I asked.

"I'm doing much better - now, especially."

"Where have you been?" I had to ask, cutting straight to the real issues.

"I needed to take some time, you know. Figure out some things."

Yeah, like the fact that you slept with a dog and gave me HIV, I wanted to blurt out. *And got your self almost killed!*

"Well, I'm glad you're okay. Umm...Gill's been

keeping me focused completed another book. I wrapped it up last week, as a matter of fact."

"Well, good. I really want to see you successful, Claude."

"Really?" I couldn't help it. My horns were definitely showing, and how dare she call after all of this time and think all is well?

"What's on your mind, Angela?"

"I want to see you," she said, like nothing had ever happened.

"Mmm-hmm... I have to get back to you on that. There's a lot going on with my folks and all, so let me get back to you."

"I'm heading out tomorrow. I was wondering if we could meet this evening?"

That silence crept in again; aloof, again, and at a complete loss for words. Gill was looking at me with those deep, penetrating eyes, and for the first time I was torn, torn between two women, torn between the past and the present.

But I needed to close this chapter. "Today? What time?" I said

"How about in a couple of hours? I'm staying at the Sterling, off 35 and Regal Row."

"OK. I will see you there in two hours."

I hung up the phone without saying goodbye, and Gill brushed past me and went outside by the pool. But I was still torn. I watched her silhouette fade out the door, Max and Moira tagging along behind her.

I went to take a shower. I knew that Gill would be there when I came back. I had to face Angela and find out the truth behind her status - and mine.

-Twenty-Four-

I managed to shower, change, and get a grip on myself while Gill stayed out of sight. I grabbed the keys to her Jeep, hoping that doing this would guarantee her being there when I returned so we could address the obvious situation that had taken place over the past year. We had fallen in love.

I drove carefully and went over in my head what I planned on saying to Angela. First, I wanted to know her status; second, how she could say she loved me and drag me into this mess; and lastly, I needed to be sure I was no longer in love with her. Or if I ever was.

The cool wind ran across my head. My shoulder-length locs seemed different now; not just an image, but a symbol of renewed strength. Not just heritage, but promise - promise to be responsible, strong, and to always live with a purpose.

I could still smell Angela...so many times, I wondered if I ever saw her again would she still smell the same...or would there be the hint of a fire smell...how would her skin look?

I pushed past downtown, slowly made my way around the curve on the freeway, then sped towards

Regal Row. I was ready to face her, ready to find out the truth. I needed the truth so I could move on.

I came to the exit rather quickly, turned left as she said, and made my way to the Sterling Hotel, just under the freeway on the right hand side. It was a modest hotel; nothing fancy. I parked and sat for a moment, reminding myself of all the answers I needed to hear.

I let myself out, walked into the hotel and went to the lounge. I then surveyed the room and saw no sign of Angela. I found a lounge chair, then flopped down, looked at my watch, and waited.

"Claude," she called from behind me, and I stood to face her.

I was shocked, and my eyes widened; she was a skeletal figure with tired eyes and tiny hands, and she looked like the weight of the world rested on her shoulders. She was a blade of grass and the glamour and glitz was gone; instead, she looked haunted...like she was at death's door. She was smoked out and looked more like a crack whore before she strolled the streets for her next high--- Her *coups de grace.* Nothing would kill her faster.

I stood there, staring at her. I wasn't just at a loss for words; I was petrified that somehow her fate was linked to mine. Her face was sunken in, and the right side was scarred. The burn covered her right temple into her hairline, ear, and jaw. Her eye had escaped, but still seemed heavy. Katrina tried to ruin her beauty. She had.

"Well, aren't you going to ask me to have a seat or join you?"

"Ahhhh, sure...sure...have a seat, Angela. How are you?" I said before reaching in for an awkward hug.

She smelled different. It was a mix between cheap shampoo, conditioner, and sweat. Her extremities showed no sign of burns, so clearly it was a crime of passion and jealousy. Her body was frail, and she felt like her bones would break into pieces if I squeezed any harder.

"Well, you look great, Claude. I like your hair. You growing them out, huh?"

She could barely remember what I looked like. When I looked deeply into her eyes, they were hazy; she was high.

"So what's been up, Angela?" I asked as we both sat down. Her mind seemed far away; she bit at her bottom lip and seemed to make a gritting motion. I could barely focus on anything but her facial movements.

"So, how's the book? Or books? I hear you're

done.”

"I am. We wrapped everything up last week, Gill and I. It's at the printer." I had had this conversation with her over the phone; strange that she was repeating it.

"So, what next?"

I wasn't sure where this was going. I thought everything had been finalized before Katrina's death and Angela's disappearance.

"Ahhhh…you tell me. Technically, you're the boss."

She looked at me strangely, and I tilted my head and looked at her.

"You did make sure the deal went through before all hell broke loose, right? The book is at the printer, Angela. Remember?"

"Gill, she's…you know…" she said, biting at that bottom lip again. "She's over everything. I signed over the company to her almost a year ago."

"Really? I wasn't aware." It didn't feel good at all that Gill had left that part out. I breathed out heavily. "So, how's your health? You find out anything?" I asked trying to hide my anger at Gill.

"Well, that's why I'm here," she said before looking away.

"Can we go somewhere private?"

"Private?"

"Yeah, you know out of the public. Where did you park?"

"Um…just outside by the tree. I'm in Gills Jeep."

"Well come on." She said moving quickly as I followed her to Gills Jeep underneath the tree.

She jumped in on the passenger side and I went to the driver side and hopped in. We sat there quiet which was awkward. She was breathing hard like we had sprinted over there. I turned to look at her when she began looking thru her purse. Her tiny hands were darker, and aged in comparison to what she once looked like. She pulled out a rolled up dollar bill, opening it and put cocaine in between her index finger and thumb, in the crevice and took a bump like it was nothing.

"Seriously?"

"I need a loan." She said in between sniffing trying to keep that tiny mountain of destruction in her nostrils.

"You need a what?" I asked. Looking at her like she said something in Chinese.

"You're not even going to hide your habit and then ask me for a loan?"

"Don't start. I don't need a mother right now."

"How long has this been going on Angela?"

She looked away embarrassed. Then faced me like I should know the answer to my own question.

"How long?" I asked again.

"Look. Things are a little tough for me. I feel like I'm right there about to turn everything around."

It was the typical addict response "I feel like it's going to get better" basically *I just need another hit until I need another hit.*

"Angela we can get you some help if that's what you need. I'm pretty sure we can get you into rehab." I said as her glassy eyes stared into mine like she hadn't heard a word I said. She looked away.

"I need a loan Claude."

"What about your health - what does that have to do with a loan?"

"Look, Claude, don't act like you don't have it; you're about to blow up, be sitting on Oprah's couch. Gill is good."

"Okay, what is this? You need a loan because I have a potential bestseller on my hand? You have a substance abuse problem and possibly infected with..."

"I just need a loan. I'm back in Cali, you know it's expensive there. I'm trying to start over."

"And so we are going to just ignore this whole cokehead label? You're an addict. You may be HIV positive. I'm not giving you shit. But I will get you some help if you want it."

"Don't judge me." She said calmly as if what she had been through validated her dance with the white horse.

"What is this, Angela?" Her eyes became serious and sad as she stared out the windshield. It was like she was about to cry and I felt bad that I was so insensitive.

"I was coming back to you---Katrina got pissed and tried to kill me because I was coming back to you."

"You, were what?" I asked moving my head in to look at her more closely.

"I was coming back. I love you. I'm in love with you. I thought maybe we could pick up where we left off."

My heart started pounding and I swear I felt light headed.

"What are you talking about? You told me you couldn't leave Katrina. You needed to be there for her. You left me high and dry and didn't bother to think about my feelings. You come back here with this. Now." I had to look away.

"You thought what?" I said, looking back at her,

"That pussy of yours is going to make me drop to my knees? And our *Shipboard Romance* in Jamaica is supposed to sustain us? You got yourself into this situation by hooking up with Katrina. This is the world you created, not mine not ours."

"So you're going to look down on me 'cause of my poor choices? You don't have that right, Claude."

"Look, I'm not trying to judge you," I said realizing her fate could have a great deal to do with me. "but I need to know about your status about being positive. That's why I'm here." She wouldn't look at me. Her hands shook as she held that wrinkled dollar bill and with out looking down, she closed it back up and wiped her nose.

"That's the only reason why you're here? That's all you care about?"

"YES." I interjected then rolling my eyes.

"What about me? WHAT THE FUCK ABOUT ME?" she shouted, getting out of the jeep and I noticed the knock-off Manolo shoes that showed strings from the cheap leather. Her legs looked worn out, like she had walked all the way to meet me at the hotel.

"I don't have a job - unless you have forgotten that,

too, Angela. So I can't just give you a loan." I said as she stood holding the door open.

"What about your house - you can't take out a loan on it?" She asked, one hand holding the door the other clutching her purse.

"Excuse me? My home is my business, and it is not going to be used for a loan - and before you raise your voice again, this conversation is finished." I looked away trying not to cry because I honestly felt sorry for her. Sorry that she didn't love herself more, that she wasn't strong and because she wasn't her life would pay the price.

She slammed the door as hard as she could and I drove off without looking back. I drove to the Health Department a couple of exits down the freeway. It was time to know my status.

238

-Twenty-Five-

Begging the guard to please let me up was of no use - I was too late. I'd have to wait until Monday morning before I could begin the journey of where my fate would lie.

My head felt heavy, and it sunk a little as I walked back to the Jeep, trying to push images of Angela from my mind. She looked a mess, and if that's where I was headed, God help me - because I was sure going to need it.

"Excuse me, miss," a young Hispanic guy called out to me.

I looked up and tried to figure out where the voice was coming from.

"Miss," he said again, and I looked over my right shoulder. He waved at me, and I nodded back.

"Do you need some assistance?"

I looked at him, this time with a frown.

"And you are...?" I asked.

"Eduardo Garcia. I work for an agency that can probably get you help today - if we hurry, of course."

"I beg your pardon?"

He walked over to me and extended his hand. "I

overheard you talking to the guard. It seems like things are pretty urgent right now. I work just down the street, and we do testing up until 7pm on Fridays and get the results back the following day."

"How much?" *Nothing's for free*, I reminded myself, *it's always some catch.*

"Actually, we are a nonprofit organization. You are more than welcome to leave a donation, if you like."

"Where is this place? And what's it called?"

"It's in the Oaklawn area, right off Oaklawn, as a matter of fact. It's called **Inspire**."

"How do I know you aren't some creep setting me up?" I had to ask. He could be one of Angela's goons, trying to rob me - seeing as though she was now destitute and obviously in need of some serious cash.

He pulled out his work ID and flashed a genuine smile.

"Oh, so you're the Director...sorry...it's just some crazy people out here."

"Tell me about it. I was just over here dropping off stats and brochures. You know the Health Department is the last place some people want to go when they are faced with this."

"Really? That's the first place I thought to go;

couldn't think of anywhere else."

"Well you're probably the first. You immediately become a statistic, labeled, and cast down. They notify past partners, have people come in; it's just ridiculous the way they handle such a personal dilemma. We try to offer privacy, assistance, and a manageable way of notifying past partners. You know, handle it all very discreetly."

I started to throw out Angela's name to see if that rang a bell, then I realized that he did say, *We handle things discreetly.*

"So, what do you say? You want to follow me there?"

"Sure. I need to get this taken care of."

"I'm parked right over there." He pointed two rows over towards the front, at a modest Honda Accord. I headed to Gill's Jeep, and we met up at the opening, right off the freeway. I followed him closely to a small building that seemed like just an ordinary building. No signs, no rainbow neon lights; just a plain two-story building next to the Wine-tasting venue.

We parked around the back and went in the employee door.

"You can wait in my office, and I'll have a counselor come in here and do the test."

I nodded my head, followed him into his office, and sat on a striped sofa that was beside a window. I was nervous, but I knew this had to be done. I let my eyes wander around his office, looking at a picture of him and his lover and two children; he looked almost ten years younger.

There were pictures of his parents, graduation, and a ribbon cutting ceremony for Inspire. Then there was one of him alone, kneeling at a gravesite, touching the headstone.

"OK," he said, walking back into the office. I jumped slightly.

"This is Tiffany; she'll be administering the test. We'll get contact information, and you'll be done. Sound okay?"

"Yes, that will be fine."

The blonde, blue-eyed woman with long wavy hair extended her hand and smiled. Compassion filled her eyes. There was no judgment; just complete and utter concern.

"If you could just rub the Q-tip around your jaw and make sure it's saturated, that would be great. Then

I'll take a blood sample, and we're done."

Eduardo excused himself, and Tiffany got right to work. She was serious and meticulous as she did everything carefully, the compassion never leaving her eyes. When she finished, she removed her gloves and shook my hand again. "We'll contact you tomorrow, either way this goes. Okay? And a brief message is a good sign. If we ask you to come back in, then you'll know that we want to test again or point you in the right direction for other resources you will need."

I knew what that meant; my ass was positive.

"Okay," I responded, and she picked up her things and let herself out, Eduardo then reappeared with a couple papers.

"All right, sweetie. You can just leave a contact phone number; we don't need your name, if you'd rather not leave it. We only report it if that's what you want. We can also link you up to many resources, even if you choose to withhold your personal information."

I took the paperwork, filled in my home phone number, and left everything else blank. Eduardo smiled, shook my hand, and said, "We'll call around noon or so tomorrow. Saturdays are our busiest days. Fridays should be, but they start the party around here by

Wednesday, and come Saturday we have tons of kids - or I should say 'people' - in here with that worried look on their faces, waiting to be tested."

"Wow. Well, I'm glad I'm here today. Don't want to be around too many people, you know; this is a very private matter," I said and let out a huge sigh. "But all I can do now is wait."

He smiled and walked me back out to Gill's Jeep. We shook hands again, then I headed back home so I could talk to Gill.

-Twenty-Six-

When I arrived home, I let up the garage door and hurried inside. I smelled sautéed onions and pepper, with a hint of Rosemary potatoes. Gill had fixed dinner.

"Gill," I called out, and Max and Moira bolted towards me, almost knocking me down.

"Gill," I called again, but there was no answer. I let the dogs out and noticed something different; my home felt empty. Aside from the smell of dinner, there was an emptiness that gave me chills.

I went to my office to see if she was working in there, then to the sitting area, to my bedroom to see if she was folding clothes or taking a nap, and finally to the spare room, where I slept.

She was gone. Her shoes, her clothes, her flip-flops, jewelry, and anything that was Gill were gone. I reached for the phone and dialed her number.

"Hi, this is Gill. Leave a message. Thanks."

"Gill, what's up? Where are you?...Ummm, is something wrong?"

I hung up, went to my room, and laid where she often slept, curling up and wondering where could she be and why had she left in such a manner. I sat up and decided I was going to find her; I had to tell her that it was her. It was her that filled me up lately and who I was glad to see every morning when we met up in my office, the kitchen, or the sitting area, talking about everything under the sun, like the impending election, stocks, the war - you name it. We were the best of friends. We were in love.

I went into my bathroom and was reaching for the faucet - when I saw a small envelope with my name on it, written in her handwriting. I opened it quickly, almost tearing the letter inside. It read:

Claude,

I've gone back home. I hope all is well with you and Angela and you two work everything out.
Love Gill

I sighed heavily, then went to the garage, hopped in my car, and headed to her place. I knew she would be there alone, now that her son was staying with his father. That was partly why she spent so much more time with me; she missed him.

Her house in Kessler Park was nice, but modest. It suited her. I parked in front, then went and rang the bell. I waited a few seconds, then the door popped open.

"Hey," I said nervously.

"Hey," she replied back, then turned to walk away as I stepped in.

"What's going on?"

"Not much. I'm about to head out to New York in about an hour. Gotta late flight. I have some early morning business to tend to."

"I thought you were going with me to pick up my father?"

"No, I can't, and that's probably something you and your mother should handle alone."

"So, you're going to New York? Just like that?"

"Yeah there's a big conference, and I'm a panel speaker."

"Really? I didn't know."

"Yeah, last minute gig. An editor friend of mine had to drop out last minute, so she passed it on to me."

"Well, that was nice."

"Yeah. Big break," she said as we walked into the kitchen. Her bags were packed already and sitting neatly beside the entrance.

"That's a lot of bags...how long are you staying?"

"For a week. Probably going to head to Atlanta from there and visit an old friend."

"Right. Right. You just decided that, too, huh?"

"Yeah, but don't worry - your book is probably going to be picked up by Doubleday. I spoke to Sandy the other day, and she said there was definitely some interest in your story. She wanted to be sure you weren't dealing with anyone else. So, our short run order to send out will be fine. We can still deliver to the local Salons."

"Oh, really? You didn't tell me."

"Well, you know I'm wearing a lot of hats right now, so I'm doing a lot - but trust: you're going to get your book deal. And besides, I wanted to wrestle your endearing piece from the hands of Angela and Katrina---it was time to put an end to their machination." I could tell she was done with Angela completely and wasn't going to come to her rescue anymore.

"I'm not worried about that, Gill." For some reason, I knew she had good reason not to tell me Angela had sold her the business. I felt completely safe with Gill yet I knew I had to ask any way.

"So, what time is your flight? You need a ride?"

"At 9:05, and no, I have a cab coming. They should be here in about twenty minutes."

"Oh, okay. So what about your Jeep? Do you want me to drop it off at the airport for you? So you can have it when you return?"

"Um...I'll let you know. I don't want to rack up unnecessary fees."

"Right." I said trying to understand her sudden change.

"So, you excited about seeing your father?"

"Not really. This is just too crazy for me."

"I can imagine."

"Yeah, and the lawyer from Jamaica; it's really weird."

She shook her head, and suddenly we were like strangers; I felt like I didn't know her...she was so distant...I couldn't put my finger on it.

"So, Angela said you're running the business now? I didn't know."

"Yep. I've been doing it for almost 10 months now. I pay her to use her name, but everything else - it's all on me."

"Wow, Gill. You gave me such attention, I didn't know you were handling all of this."

"Yeah, that's part of why my son went to stay with his father. You know Angela and Katrina left a huge mess with this business, debtors, unpaid bills and so on. I've been cleaning it up, for the most part. Your book is probably the only legit thing they did do."

"I guess that's why she thinks I owe her. She asked for a loan today!"

"Are you serious?"

"As a heart attack."

"I can't believe her. I just paid her the monthly fee for her name usage the other day."

"You talked to her?"

"No, it's handled through the banks. I was just as shocked to hear from her as you. She told me she was moving back to California when we closed the deal."

"She doesn't throw those big parties anymore? You know the Women's Mixer? She gave that up too?"

"Angela didn't *throw* those parties in the first place. Chick Happy hour is sponsored by a wealthy banker who felt Dallas needed a social event for lesbians that were classy Angela and Katrina rolled in and *pretended* like they were throwing those parties."

"Are you kidding me?"

"Not kidding."

"Wow---what was she being truthful about? Jeez! Well she's supposedly in California now--- but who knows."

"Yeah, she lives out there. She was in town, I guess, or is in town because she wanted to see me for a loan. I suppose." Gill looked away. I noticed her discomfort; something was bothering her.

"So why didn't you tell me?"

"Tell you what?"

"About the company and buying her out, and the name usage? I mean, we've been working so close together---how could you leave that out?"

"It wasn't intentional or superficial if that's what you're asking.---I didn't want you to worry."

"You know I trust you. Right? I know you're real."

"Well, thank you. I have no reason not to be."

"And you're right, this isn't superficial."

"No it isn't."

There was a silence that settled in and I just could not bring myself to say anymore. Angela's request and her admittance about leaving Katrina had my head all mixed up. A part of me wanted to save her. Resurrect her.

"Well, I gotta finish up around here. I'll call you when I get there."

"Gill..." I said earnestly. "I'm going to miss you." She smiled and her eyes seemed to well up.

"I'll miss you. too. I'll call you." she said and asked that I let myself out. She went one way, and I went the opposite - towards the door. I grabbed the handle, then turned to look back for her. She wasn't there; she was gone.

-Twenty-Seven-

I slept through the next day, ignoring the chirping sounds of my answering machine, and fate. Getting up to let Max and Moira out, give them food and water, and use the rest room was all I could muster up enough courage to do. On six o'clock Sunday morning, I finally got up to shower, then headed to my mother's after staring at the blinking lights on the answering machine that seemed to moved rapidly like it was an urgent message there. But I wasn't going to check it until I talked to my mother first.

It was time that I prepared her for my past transgressions.

As I pulled up, Julia was heading out in her little two-seater.

"Good morning, Sunshine," she said in her authentic accent.

"Good morning, Superstar," I said back.

"I'm glad to see that your ladder is being repaired."

"It is; I'm on my way up."

"Yes, you are - just don't think you have to get there alone."

I smiled. "I don't. I'm taking you and Mom with me. We gon' be like the Jefferson's, *moving' on up!"* I sang.

"Not exactly what I had in mind, Claude." She winked, "Don't forget about the ones that helped you get to where you are; those that helped with the repair job."

"I won't. Are you coming back later?"

"We'll see. Your mom has some things to take care of. I don't want to get in the way."

I nodded, then waved as she drove off. My mother was choosing my Dad over Julia, again...crazy.

"Mom," I called out as I pushed open the door.

"I'm in the kitchen," she called back.

"Good morning," I said as I approached her and walked over to kiss her soft cheeks. Her back was to me, and she was still in her robe.

"Hey, sweetheart," she said.

"You OK? I just saw Julia leaving."

"I'm fine. We just had a little talk, is all. But I'm fine."

She faced me, wiping her eyes. She was saddened by her decision.

"Mom, if you love her, don't let her go."

"It's not that simple."

"Yes, it is. Dad coming back is not your problem."

"How could you say something so silly, Claude?

That's my husband and your father."

"Mom, Dad's a fraud."

"A what?"

"A fraud. He has a whole other family in Jamaica - and did you know he let Uncle Peter die alone because he was gay? He was ashamed of his own family, and he's ashamed of me, too. He isn't my father."

"Claude, stop it right this minute!" she said sternly.

"Mom, I'm telling you; he treated me like crap when I went home with him to see Uncle Peter, then he tells me about all of these brothers and sisters I have. It's fuckin' ridiculous. He's a hypocrite and a liar."

"You watch your mouth, young lady; that is still your father. And is this the news you wanted to share with me? This is rather hurtful, Claude, and very inconsiderate."

"Mom, I don't want you to be his fool anymore. You deserve to be happy and with someone who loves you."

"Why? So I won't wind up like you - pining over some beauty queen that almost took you for every dime you had? You're so superficial, Claude. I don't know where you've picked that up. Honestly."

"Are you talking about Angela? I'm not with her,

nor do I want her. And this isn't about me; I'm trying to help you."

"Well, I don't need your help, Claude. I have every right to love and miss your father. This nonsense about Jamaica stops now - do you hear me?" she said, raising her voice and balling her hands up at her side.

"Mom -"

"NOW, Claude! It stops now!"

I rolled my eyes to the top of my head, looked away, and then turned to look at my mother, trying to understand exactly what she was doing.

"What about Julia? You're willing to forget about her and just go back to 'normal?'" I said, using my hands and fingers to make my point. I felt like a hypocrite now.

"Julia and I are none of your business - and before you decide to put me on your 'team,' we are just friends. I've been Julia's only family ever since she was cast out and abandoned by her own. I love her, but not as she wishes, or as you think. I've been going around the country, crusading for her, for my daughter, and countless other lesbians who deserve a voice - not for US! So, if you're finished here, I'll see you at the airport."

"Wait, Mom; there's something else."

She looked at me like she couldn't bear to hear

another story about my father. It was all over her face; my words had cut her deeply, and she just wanted me to stop.

"It's me, Mom…I've been keeping something from you."

"Go on," she said, her eyes welling up with tears.

"I don't know how to say this." I breathed out and let my eyes become moist. I needed a real cry; I needed my mother to wipe these tears away. She walked over to me and grabbed my hand.

"Sweetheart, what is it?"

"I may…" I paused. My heart was heavy in my chest, and my throat dried up like a barren land. "I'm possibly HIV-positive."

The words seemed to echo throughout the kitchen. I looked away out of shame; my mother said nothing, probably out of confusion.

"What happened, sweetheart? Was it some medical emergency you didn't mention? Did you have a transfusion and get tainted blood? What happened? Sweetie, what's going on?" she asked, holding my hand as I turned away and let the tears fall from my eyes. I was more hurt by my irresponsibility than anything. How I let myself get caught up with the likes of Angela made me feel like a real piece a crap. From her touch, I felt my mother's pain. She was going to have to care for me and my mess, and she didn't deserve the news that I'd been harboring and now dropped on her.

I let go of her hand and wiped my eyes. I then turned to face her and began telling her the truth.

"Angela. Angela's ex was a heroine addict, or user. She infected Angela, and Angela could have given it to me."

"Could have? Are you sure, or not? I'm not understanding."

"I took the test, and the results are in; I just have to get them from the answering machine. They came in yesterday...I'm scared...I'm scared, Mom." I cried uncontrollably and melted into my mother's arms. Fragilely, she tried to hold me up, almost like she was telling me that I needed to be strong, that now was not the time for either of us to fall apart.

"Sweetheart, look at me," she said, forcing me to pull it together and look at her. "You have got to find out the truth."

"I can't...I can't," I said in-between sobs. With saliva dripping from my mouth and snot dangling from my nose, I used my hand to wipe it away.

"Yes. You can. You will. There are tons of agencies and resources for HIV-infected women, and, being a lesbian, surely there are resources to help you."

"I just want to die, Mom; I can't live like this."

"No, no - you are not a coward. We didn't raise you to be one. Now, we're going to pick up your father and get those results immediately afterwards. Do you hear me?"

I looked away and wiped my hand on my pants leg.

"Look at me, Claudette; we are going to get through this." She grabbed me and hugged me tight, holding me for some time. I hoped she was praying because I surely was.

She let me go, wiped her eyes, and said, "I'm going to get dressed; be back in a sec."

My head felt like elephants had trampled on it. I needed some coffee, so I fixed myself a cup, then sat and drank and wondered about how to tell Gill, as well as how my father would treat me now.

"I'm ready," Mom said as she reappeared in the kitchen, looking radiant.

"Julia's going to meet us there. Come on."

I followed behind her, and as we drove we listened to talk radio in my mother's Volvo.

"How's Gill?" she asked, busting up the silence.

"Gone to New York on business…distant."

"Does she know?"

"No. I haven't told anyone except you."

"What does Angela have to say for herself?"

"She's strung out; clueless about everything."

"Is she?"

"Yeah. I saw her a few days ago, and she looked awful. I couldn't get a straight answer from her. All she wanted was more money for drugs."

"And Katrina…she's passed, right?"

"Yeah. Suicide."

"Hmmm…and Gill's take on all of this?"

"She doesn't say much either. She has the agency now and pays Angela for the name usage, but she didn't even tell me that. She's been cleaning it up, is what she said, but nothing about Angela is ever mentioned."

"Well, do you plan on telling her?"

"Yes." I wanted to say more, but I wasn't sure if she was still talking about my status or my feelings for Gill.

"I think you should. That's most important right now."

"Yes, ma'am."

The news commentator came back on with news about the impending election. Something about Barack being bad for the country and McCain representing change. It's funny how people's perspectives could be so twisted, even with all the facts staring them in the face.

We pulled up to the airport and went to the American Airlines terminal. Julia was waiting out front, and the three of us walked in and waited by the gate and baggage claim area for my father to arrive. Probably not the homecoming he would prefer, but, strangely enough, I felt a bit more relaxed.

"I see some people coming out," Julia said, and we all stood like this great wall of sisterhood, basically ready for my father to face the music.

One by one, people trickled out, and when it seemed like there were no more people, two officers opened the doors by the revolving gate and pushed a wooden box through them. They seemed to be looking for someone, then looked at us and said, "Are you the Moore's?"

Dad was dead.

He'd hung himself after talking to me and Mom. The woman that was supposed to meet us there showed up as Mom was signing the slip.

"Mrs. Moore," she called out in her polished accent. "I'm Ms. Trina Thomas. Your husband has asked that I give you some things."

My mother was quiet and looked at the woman as she went on. "The first is the name of his cellmate, Kevin. He said Claudette would know what to do with his story. The second, information regarding property in Jamaica - it has been transferred to your name. Lastly, his journal. He wanted you to have it."

I reached for it before my mother could; I knew she wasn't ready for the truth. Grabbing Julia's hand, she turned and walked out, and I was left standing there with a pine box and my father's journal.

It was Sunday. Who picks up the dead on a Sunday? I went to the pay phone, put in some change, and called the City Morgue, who in turn gave me the number to a mortician. I then sat and proceeded to wait for three hours.

While I waited, I read page after page of my father's torture in a Jamaican prison and how some kid named Kevin was wrongfully accused and rotting away in jail for a crime he did not commit. He went on about me knowing what to do to help this kid and that he was proud that I was his daughter and a talented writer whose stories would change the world. He said over and over again, "Help Kevin. Help Kevin. Please help Kevin."

When they finally picked him up, the story of Kevin was etched in every part of my brain and memory. I had to help him. I grabbed a cab back to my place, found the spare key underneath the floor pot, and let myself in. I ran my hands through my hair and thought about the strength that was holding me together as I walked to the kitchen.

"Claude," she said softly, and I peeked into the kitchen and saw Gill smiling at me.

"Hey, you," I smiled back, and she walked over to me, wrapped her arms around me, and let her body resurrect mine. She then whispered in my ear, "It's negative, baby. The test results are negative."

I looked into her eyes and kissed her passionately, savoring her, loving her, and accepting that my ladder had finally been repaired.

"I'm in love with you." I said looking deep into her eyes.

"I'm in love with you too." She said as time stood still and our souls connected on so many levels. She was my friend, my partner my soul mate and the love of my life.

Gills hand reached for mine, and she intertwined our hands then led me to my room. Her suitcase was beside the door and we both looked down at the significance of it being here in my bedroom, our bedroom. She pulled my hand up to her caramel lips they were perfect and kissed the center of my hand. Her eyes, the same doe eyes that had caught my attention at our first meeting, the same ones that always sat and listened, the same ones that I could see underneath her mask at the masquerade party and the same ones that were filled with so much hurt when I came back from Angela were now spilling over with tears of joy.

I placed my free hand on her face, examining her natural beauty and gently wiped away her tears while tears of my own trickled down my cheeks. Instead of moans from love making there were sobs, sobs of joy that we had each other. We had love. True love.

The End

If you enjoyed Broken Ladder, check out an excerpt from novelist, T.R.A.D.E (Telling Real Ass Dirty Escapades), entitled Little Boi Blu. It's a gritty narrative told through the eyes of Blu, a male hustler living by his own rules in the heart of Pleasant Grove, Dallas. He decides to take in homeless Courtney - a 17-year-old pretty boy. His decision is costly, as Courtney has a hustle of his own.

ONE

My name is Blu. No last name, no middle initial, and nothing fancy to address who I am. And furthermore, I don't give a fuck what you call me - just bend yo' ass ova when I give you the cue. Once I lick my lips, I'ma split yo ass open, just like you like it.

I don't have a heart. I'm ruthless, and, after I screw you, you better believe I'm hitting your pockets, too. I live in D-Town, better known as Dallas. I thug in Oak cliff, screw rich white boys in up-town, church boys on Sunday, and married men all through the week.

My apartment in Pleasant Grove is laced with all the finest; things that were given to me, and most things that I've took. By the time you finished reading my story, you'll think, "Damn! That's a bad muthafucka!" But I ain't interested in no mommas, pussy, or anything that remotely reminds me of fish. That shit stinks!

However, my life was going fine until Courtney showed up. His pretty ass turned my life upside down, in more ways than one.

My problems however all started when I went against the tiny morsel of a brain I have and let that little bastard live with me. I felt sorry for ol' dude, and because

I wasn't ever going to bang his back out, I thought the least I could do was give him a place to stay after seeing him so many nights roaming the streets or begging for some money to get something to eat.

I literally watched this little boy grow up from being probably age ten until now -17.

His momma was the neighborhood crack head, who sold most of her kids right off her hip, except Courtney - who I suspect served as his mother's bait and switch. He always flirted with me, but it didn't matter because the one thing I didn't screw besides pussy was little boys or twinks or whatever the fuck they were calling themselves these days.

His mother finally died about a month ago from AIDS, Hep C, and anything else that would cause a body to stop working; but Courtney, he was pretty: built, and not a blemish on his face. He was dark chocolate with wavy hair and a look about him that suggested that he was twenty-seven instead of seventeen. I told him he could stay if he was clean from any drugs - including weed - kept his dick clean, and stayed out of my business. He agreed.

But I should have known any person that would trick out their own momma to support a crack habit was

ruthless, a hustler, and more trouble than I could
handle.